WEST OF THE BIG RIVER

THE LAWMAN

D1739176

Western Fictioneers Presents

West of the Big River

The Lawman

A Novel Based on the Life of
William Tilghman

by

James Reasoner

Western Fictioneers

For Kit Prate who came up with
the idea for West of the Big River.

Chapter 1

Oklahoma Territory, 1893

The gunshot in the distance made the man hunkered on his heels next to the creek look up. Without him having to think about what he was doing, his right hand moved a little closer to the butt of the Colt .45 holstered on his right hip.

He stood up, uncoiling smoothly to his full height, and gazed through the cottonwood trees along the banks at the riders coming quickly toward the stream. He counted three of them.

If they were looking for trouble, three against one odds weren't very good. He didn't believe in jumping to conclusions, though, and he didn't believe in running, either, so instead of jumping on his horse and lighting a shuck out of there, he stayed where he was and waited for the men to come to him.

Their loud talk and laughter drifted over the prairie to the man beside the creek. Their boisterous attitude hinted that the man who'd fired the single shot had done so in sheer exuberance, rather than for any sinister reason. They might be cowboys just blowing off steam.

When they were about fifty yards away, they must have noticed the man and his horse for the first time. They slowed their mounts but didn't stop, approaching the creek at a more deliberate, cautious pace.

They also spread out a little, making it more difficult for a lone man to do battle with them in a gunfight. That meant they weren't babes in the woods, the man mused.

His left hand was a little wet, so he dried it on his trousers. He wasn't sweating. He had just used that hand to scoop up some creek water and drink it when he heard the shot.

If any of the men saw the gesture and wanted to take it as an indication that he was nervous, that was fine, he thought. That might make them underestimate him. He was always thinking about things like that, about ways to gain any advantage, no matter how small.

Such habits were how he had stayed alive this long.

The riders came to a stop on the other side of the creek, about twenty feet away. They were young, not much out of their teens, but they already had a hard look about them. Their casual demeanor made it plain that while they were interested in the stranger, they weren't afraid of him. He looked to be almost twice as old as them. They had the superiority of youth, as well as numbers.

The middle one, who had a round, sunburned face, edged his horse a little ahead of the others.

"Waterin' your horse?" he asked.

"That's right," the lone man said. "And getting a drink myself, as well as enjoying the shade of these cottonwoods for a few minutes. The sun's a mite warm today."

"Yeah, it is. Gonna be a hot summer, I bet. That's what the woollyworms tell me, anyway. You got a name, mister?"

"You can call me Bill."

"Pleased to meet you, Bill." The spokesman didn't offer his name or those of his companions. "Where are you headed?"

"A town called Burnt Creek," Bill replied. "You know it?"

"Heard of it. Don't know that I've ever been

there. Fifty or sixty miles west of here, ain't it?"

"Not quite that far."

"You got business there?"

"That's right."

"And what sort of business would that be?"

With a faint smile on his lips under the sweeping brown mustache, Bill said dryly, "Mine."

One of the other men stiffened and leaned forward in the saddle as if he took offense at that answer, but the spokesman lifted a hand in a signal for him to take it easy.

The spokesman laughed a little and said, "We like to mind our own business, too. All right if we water our horses?"

Bill waved his left hand toward the creek.

"Help yourself. It's not my water."

"Reckon it belongs to Uncle Sam. This is all federal grazin' land through here, I believe. But I don't figure he'll miss a little of it."

The men dismounted. Bill took note of how they did it one at a time, so that somebody was always watching him. All three men carried handguns, and rifles stuck up from saddle scabbards on two of the horses. They were well-armed and had the look of men who knew how to use the weapons.

So did Bill. He was tall, with the rangy body of a frontiersman. His hair was brown under a broad-brimmed, cream-colored hat with a round crown. He habitually carried his head cocked just slightly to the left, as if he were watching and listening for anything unusual.

The .45 on his hip had walnut grips that were worn smooth in places from use. He had a Winchester on his saddle as well. The three men wouldn't have missed seeing these things, and despite their youth they knew to be wary.

The spokesman continued making small talk as the horses drank, saying, "Where are you from?"

"I was at Guthrie last," Bill said. "Born in Iowa, though. Grew up in Kansas."

"We're from Texas."

The twang in the man's voice had been enough to tell Bill that.

"Went up the trail with a few herds," the spokesman went on. "Then we decided we'd eaten enough dust and stared at enough cow rear ends to last a lifetime, so we set out to wander around a bit."

"A footloose life can be a good one," Bill said. "I've always been a bit restless myself. Tried plenty of things, but if they didn't get me out in the country enough, I soon grew tired of them."

"I understand. What are you doin' these days, if you don't mind me askin'."

Bill edged aside the lapel of his coat so that the badge pinned to his shirt was revealed.

One of the other men ripped out a curse and reached for his gun. He stopped short of grabbing it when he saw that Bill's hand was already resting on his Colt.

"Settle down, Asa," the spokesman quickly told his friend. "We don't want any trouble." He looked at Bill and went on, "Your last name wouldn't be Tilghman, would it, amigo?"

"It would."

"Well, hell. All this open space out here, and who do we ride up on but a deputy U.S. marshal?"

"That's the way luck goes sometimes," Bill Tilghman said. "You boys wanted for anything?"

"Don't answer him, Todd," the one called Asa said quickly. "He's tryin' to trick you."

"Seems like a pretty straightforward question to me," Tilghman drawled. "The answer's either yes or no."

"If I say yes," Todd said, "are you gonna try to arrest us?"

"Depends on whether or not they're federal

charges." Tilghman frowned in thought. "Also, I really need to get on to Burnt Creek as soon as I can. I don't really have time to go back to the territorial capital at Guthrie with three prisoners."

"You sound mighty confident that you'll take us in, mister," Asa snapped.

"Well, that's my job, arresting criminals and taking them back to be dealt with by the law. If I wasn't confident that I could do the job, I never would've pinned on this badge. It's like when I was hunting buffalo. I knew I was a good shot and could drop one of those beasts from long range. I missed now and then, but not often."

Todd licked his lips and said, "We're not wanted on any federal charges, Marshal."

"I hope you're not lying to me," Tilghman said. "If I was to get back to Guthrie after this little chore in Burnt Creek is taken care of and ask around about three young fellows, one named Todd, another named Asa, and the other one . . . well, I don't expect you to tell me, but I could find out easy enough. Anyway, if I was to find out that you were federal fugitives, I wouldn't take it kindly that you lied to me. I'd have to go and look you up and let you know I wasn't happy about it."

"You won't have any reason to look us up," Todd said. "I swear it." He was pale now, and sweat had broken out on his forehead. Tilghman's unshakable, deadly calm had that effect on men.

"All right," Tilghman said with a nod. He reached for his horse's dangling reins with his left hand. Turning the animal so that its body was between him and the three men on the other side of the creek, he swung up into the saddle.

The third man, the one whose name he didn't know, thought about reaching for his revolver. Tilghman saw that in his eyes. But the man hesitated, drew in a deep breath, blew it out, and lifted his hand away from his gun.

Tilghman nodded again and heeled his horse into motion. The animal's hooves splashed in the water as Tilghman rode across the creek. He angled away from the stream so that he could still see the three men from the corner of his eye.

They mounted up, pounded across the creek, and rode eastward in a hurry.

Another faint smile tugged at Tilghman's lips. He didn't like drawing his gun and never did it unless he had no choice. But he would if he had to, and most men on the wrong side of the law here in Oklahoma Territory had heard of him and knew that.

He had a hunch that he wouldn't get out of Burnt Creek without unleathering that .45.

Chapter 2

Evett Nix was the chief United States Marshal for the Oklahoma Territory. With his sober suits, slicked-down hair parted in the middle, and neatly trimmed mustache, he looked more like a businessman than a lawman, which was fitting because that was exactly what he'd been before President Grover Cleveland put him in charge of law and order for the Territory.

Nix might not have had much experience at being a star packer, but he knew how to judge men's character and how to work effectively with them. He wanted a certain type of individual for his deputies: cool under fire, not inclined to recklessness or grandstanding, intelligent, and good enough with gun, knife, and fist to stay alive in a country full of badmen.

Bill Tilghman was the perfect example of that type.

He had been a cowboy and buffalo hunter as a young man, before drifting into law work. Since then he had served as the under-sheriff in Dodge City, working under the famous Bat Masterson, whom Tilghman had known in their buffalo hunting days, then as sheriff and finally as city marshal of that notorious cowtown. At every step along the way, Tilghman had been successful at strengthening the forces of law and order.

That was why Evett Nix had tapped him as a deputy U.S. marshal. Now Tilghman could use his talents and determination to help bring the law to an entire territory that was rife with lawlessness.

A couple of days before the encounter with the three young cowboys, Nix had called Tilghman into his office in the federal building in Guthrie, the territorial capital.

"I'm sending you to a town called Burnt Creek, Bill," Nix said. "You know it?"

Tilghman nodded.

"It's out toward the panhandle. A year ago it wasn't much more than just a wide place in the trail. I've heard it's grown a lot since then. One of the cattle trails leading to Colorado goes through there. The herds stop because there's a good place to water them along the creek and it's well-situated for resting the stock for a few days before pushing along with the rest of the drive."

"That's right," Nix said. "Cattle made it grow, and cattle keeps it alive and prosperous. Some people don't seem to understand that, though."

Tilghman frowned slightly, adjusted the hat he had hung on a knee when he sat down in front of Nix's desk and crossed his legs, and said, "You'll have to explain that."

"Rustlers have started working the area. Half a dozen herds have been hit. Seven men are dead, and quite a few have been wounded during the raids. There's talk that the herds may start taking a different trail. That's not all. Travelers have been waylaid and robbed. It's gotten bad enough that a number of citizens have complained to the governor, and he's asked for federal help."

"That would be me," Tilghman drawled.

"That would be you," Nix agreed with a smile. "I'd sent Madsen and Thomas with you, but they're both busy with other assignments right now. As soon as they come back in, I'll send them after you to give you a hand, if you need it."

Tilghman nodded. He would have been happy to have Chris Madsen and Heck Thomas accompany him to Burnt Creek. They were fellow deputy U.S. marshals, and more importantly, they were Tilghman's friends and mighty good men to have at your side in a fight. But if they weren't available right now to help him, then so be it. Tilghman wasn't in the habit of turning down assignments, no matter how tough they might be.

"I reckon I can handle it," he told Nix. "Is there any law already in Burnt Creek?"

"Just a city marshal, name of Dave Rainey. I don't know anything about him, but you probably can't count on him for much help. His jurisdiction ends at the edge of town. I doubt if he's good for anything more than arresting drunks. Most city officers aren't." Nix chuckled. "You were an exception, Bill."

"Well, maybe he can give me some information, anyway. I'll go take a look around. Some of the people who live in the area are bound to know something about that gang of rustlers."

"It's a matter of getting them to talk to you."

Tilghman grunted. He knew Nix was right about that. Many of the settlers who lived on outlying farms and ranches provided food, sanctuary, and fresh horses for the badmen who roamed the territory. Some did so because they were related to the outlaws, others because they admired those desperadoes, but most of them cooperated simply because they were scared something bad would happen to them and their families if they didn't. More than one ranch house had been burned out mysteriously in the middle of the night.

"Anything else?" Tilghman asked.

"No. I trust you'll figure out the best way to proceed once you're there. You've gone after outlaws like this before. I trust your judgement, Bill."

Tilghman stood up, holding his hat in his left hand. He extended his right across the desk and shook with the chief marshal. The assignment was a simple one: bring the outlaws plaguing the area around Burnt Creek to justice, whether that meant arresting them . . . or some other disposition.

Simple to describe, but maybe not so easy to do.

As he rode toward Burnt Creek now, Tilghman thought about Todd, Asa, and the other young man he had met earlier. There was a chance they were part of the gang he was after. He knew that, and yet he had let them go.

For one thing, they were riding away from Burnt Creek. That meant they must have left the gang, if indeed they'd ever been mixed up with it. For another, although Tilghman would have shot it out with them if he'd had to, the odds would have been against him. He probably would have been wounded, maybe even killed. And the job he'd been sent here to do would be over before it even got started.

A lawman had to bide his time, strike when the moment was right. Otherwise he'd be risking his life foolishly.

A thread of smoke climbing into the blue sky ahead of him caught Tilghman's attention. It looked like it was coming from somebody's chimney. Even though he was still quite a distance from the settlement of Burnt Creek, he might stop at the farm or ranch he was approaching and see if he could find out anything useful. The people who lived there probably wouldn't suspect anything if he asked permission to water his horse. While he was there he would ask a few carefully worded questions.

The house came into view a few minutes later. Like most dwellings out here on these mostly treeless plains it was made from blocks of sod cut into squares and stacked up to form walls. One side had been hollowed out of a rise, and a thatched roof was laid on top of it. Houses like this were always damp, but they were fairly warm in the winter and cool in the summer, and most importantly, they were the best that the settlers could do.

A corral was built out of posts probably hauled in from the trees along the creek Tilghman had crossed miles back. It held a milk cow and a team of mules that the farmer used for plowing. A vegetable garden was planted near the house. Farther away fields of wheat and corn were visible.

Living here would be a hardscrabble existence, but a man might make a go of it if he and his family were willing to work diligently enough. There were worse ways to live, thought Tilghman.

His eyes narrowed slightly at the sight of two saddle horses tied in front of the soddy.

Animals like that didn't belong here. The farmer already had visitors.

A big yellow cur came bounding to meet him, barking loudly along the way. That announced his arrival just as effectively as if he'd been ringing a cowbell. So much for riding up without anybody knowing he was coming. But that didn't really matter, he told himself. He wasn't one to sneak around, anyway.

As Tilghman reined in about twenty yards from the soddy's open door, a man slouched into view. He wore lace-up work boots, canvas trousers, and had suspenders hung over bony shoulders clad in the uppers of a pair of long underwear. Dark stubble on lean cheeks testified that his face hadn't known a razor for at least a week. His dark hair was in disarray. He jerked his head in a nod and called to Tilghman, "Howdy."

"Afternoon," Tilghman replied. "I see you've got a well over there. Mind if I avail myself of some water for my horse?"

"Go ahead," the man said. His voice was curt and unfriendly, but nobody turned away travelers out here.

Tilghman heeled his mount into a walk, angling toward the well. The farmer came out of the house and picked up an ax that was leaning against the sod wall. He ambled in Tilghman's direction. Tilghman had his right hand on his thigh, not far from his gun. If the man made a move to attack with that ax, Tilghman planned to shoot him. You couldn't take chances with something like that.

As the man came closer, though, Tilghman noticed something about him. He wasn't as hostile as Tilghman had thought at first. That wasn't anger lurking in the man's eyes.

It was fear.

Tilghman dismounted beside the low stone wall around the well. The farmer was only about ten feet away now. Quietly enough that he wouldn't be heard inside the soddy, Tilghman asked, "Something wrong, friend?"

The man's prominent adam's apple bobbed up and down as he swallowed.

"You gotta just water your horse and ride on, mister," he said, keeping his voice equally as quiet. "And if I talk rough to you, please don't pay it no never-mind. It's just that I got to."

Tilghman started pulling the bucket up from the well.

"You've got two men inside the house you don't want to be there," he said. "I can see that. I'd be glad to help you – "

"I don't need no help," the farmer cut in. "Best thing you can do for me is to ride on, like I said. They'll leave, too, in a little while, once they've got what they came for."

"What's that? Coffee? Some hot food? Whiskey?"

"I don't have no whiskey. They just asked my woman to fix 'em a meal. That's all. They won't bother us."

Tilghman held the bucket so his horse could drink out of it. He said, "They're part of the bunch that's been rustling cattle and causing so much trouble hereabouts, aren't they?"

The farmer let out a low moan.

"Oh, Lord," he whispered. "You're a lawman, aren't you? Please just ride on. They'll kill her if you don't."

"What are their names?" Tilghman asked. "Who's in charge of the gang? Tell me something that'll help me, and I won't cause trouble for you and your missus."

The man licked his lips and said, "I can't tell you. It'd get back to – "

Before he could go on, another man stepped out of the soddy. He yelled, "I know you, by God! You're Tilghman!"

His hand clawed at the revolver on his hip.

Chapter 3

In a gunfight, there was a big difference between hurrying and not wasting any time. The man who hurried usually died.

Tilghman didn't waste any time. He tossed the bucket aside, used his left hand to shove the farmer to the ground as he pivoted, and drew the Colt .45.

The man in the doorway already had his gun out, but he fired without taking the time to aim. The bullet whined past Tilghman on the left, missing him by several yards.

Tilghman thrust his arm out and aimed the Colt. Firing from the hip was just too inaccurate. The gun roared as he squeezed the trigger.

The man in the doorway went over backward as the slug smashed into his chest. Tilghman knew that when a man was hit like that, he didn't get up again.

But there were two horses tied up out here, and the farmer had said there was more than one man inside. As Tilghman stepped to the side, putting his horse between him and the soddy, he told the farmer, "Crawl behind the well. You ought to be safe there."

"My wife – " the man gasped.

"He won't hurt her," Tilghman said. "Now get behind the well!"

The farmer scrambled for cover. Tilghman took hold of his mount's reins with his left hand and tightened his grip on them to make the horse stand still. He laid the .45's barrel across the saddle, aimed at the house.

"Throw out your guns and then come out with your hands up!" he called. "No need for anybody else to get hurt."

For a long moment no response came from inside the soddy. Then a man shouted, "You can go straight to hell, mister! You throw your guns down and ride away, or else I'll kill this sodbuster's wife!"

From behind the low wall of the well, the farmer begged, "Please do what he wants, Marshal Tilghman. He'll kill her, I know he will! Nobody crosses this bunch."

"You know who I am?"

"I heard the one you shot call you by name, and well, everybody in this part of the country has heard of Bill Tilghman."

Tilghman's mouth tightened under his mustache. A reputation was a two-edged sword for a lawman. Sometimes it helped in talking an outlaw into giving up, but sometimes it just fueled their determination not to surrender.

"You know I can't do that," he told the farmer. "That man in there is a criminal and he's probably threatening your woman with a gun right now. I can't let him get away with that."

"You already killed one of 'em. Ain't that enough?"

No, thought Tilghman. No, it wasn't.

But he didn't expect a man whose wife was in danger to understand that.

"Come out here where I can see you," he called into the shadowy interior of the soddy. "For all I know you're all trying to trick me and there's no woman in there."

"There is!" the farmer yelped. "I swear it, Marshal, he's got my wife."

"Shut up," Tilghman said under his breath without looking away from the doorway.

The farmer still had hold of the ax. He got up

on his hands and knees, finding the courage somewhere to say, "You get on out of here like he told you, Marshal, or I'll come after you with this ax."

"Try something foolish like that and I'll have to shoot you, too."

"But if you turn to shoot me, he'll shoot you. And if you don't, I'll chop your head open."

"You'll be on the run from the law for the rest of your life if you do that."

"Yeah, but she'll still be alive."

Tilghman couldn't argue with that logic.

The farmer went on in a miserable voice, "I'm sorry, Marshal. I don't want it to be like this, I truly don't. But you can't cross that Rainey bunch. They're all cold-blooded killers."

As if to prove the man's point, two figures appeared in the doorway. The one in front was a woman, as worn-down and haggard from prairie life as her husband. The man behind her had his left arm around her neck. His right hand held a gun with the barrel digging into her side. He forced her to step over the body of the man Tilghman had shot as they moved into the open.

The farmer gasped in horror at the sight.

"Take a good look!" the outlaw told Tilghman. "You see how scared she is, Marshal? She knows I'll kill her if you don't drop your gun."

"I drop my gun and you'll kill me," Tilghman said. "But if you shoot that poor woman, you won't have a shield anymore and I'll put a bullet in you. The only way nobody dies is for you to let her go, throw your gun down, and surrender."

"How do I know you wouldn't just shoot me the way you did Jack?"

"Because I'm a lawfully appointed and sworn federal officer. I don't gun down prisoners."

"Don't reckon I feel like takin' that chance." The outlaw prodded the gun even harder into the woman's side, making her gasp in pain. She arched her back, but his grip was too tight for her to pull away.

That was more than her husband could stand. He surged up from behind the well, lifting the ax as he lunged at Tilghman. Tilghman swung the horse around to block the farmer's attack, but that opened him up to the outlaw, who let go of the woman, jerked the gun up, and fired at Tilghman.

Once more haste was a man's undoing. The bullet burned a path across the top of the horse's rump, behind the saddle, but that was as close as it came to Tilghman. He snapped his gun back into line and fired. The bullet punched into the outlaw's midsection and doubled him over. He stayed on his feet for a moment and even tried to lift the gun for a second shot, but his strength deserted him and he pitched forward on his face.

The pain of being creased had spooked Tilghman's horse. The animal danced around and forced the farmer to scurry backward to keep from being trampled. The man tripped and sprawled on his backside, dropping the ax. Tilghman took a quick step and picked it up, then swung back toward the man he had just wounded. Gut-shot men usually didn't die right away, and in his book an outlaw who wasn't either unconscious or dead was still a threat.

With the Colt leveled in one hand and the ax in the other, Tilghman strode toward the fallen man. The outlaw had dropped his gun when he fell. Tilghman kicked it away, well out of reach. The wounded outlaw was curled in a ball around the awful pain in his middle. A dark red pool spread slowly on the thirsty ground where he lay.

Tilghman hooked a boot toe under the man's shoulder and rolled him onto his back. The man shuddered, and his open, staring eyes turned glassy. He was gone.

The man in the doorway was dead, too. Tilghman had been confident of that, but he checked anyway. He took his first good look at the man's face, which was familiar. After a moment Tilghman came up with the name: Jack Culbertson. He'd arrested Culbertson for armed robbery while serving as the marshal of Dodge City.

Obviously Culbertson hadn't forgotten him, either, and the grudge he carried had prompted him into the foolish decision to come out of the soddy and try to settle the old score face to face.

He'd have been better off just shooting through the open door and killing Tilghman without warning.

Hurried footsteps made the lawman tighten his grip on the Colt and glance around. Nobody was attacking him now, though. The farmer ran to his wife, who had fallen to the ground and lay there sobbing. He dropped to his knees beside her and grabbed her, lifting her and hauling her into his lap.

"Are you all right? Are you hurt?"

She said something incoherent and kept crying. Tilghman didn't see any blood on her dress and figured she wasn't wounded, just scared out of her wits. He bent down, took hold of Jack Culbertson's ankle, and dragged the outlaw's body out of the doorway.

"You ought to take her inside, settle her down, maybe get her something to drink," he told the farmer.

The man looked up at him. He was crying, too. The tears had cut trenches in the permanent grime on his face.

"I'm sorry, Marshal," he said, sounding as wretched as he looked. "I . . . I just lost my head. I was so scared . . . Are you gonna arrest me?"

"For what?" Tilghman asked gruffly. "Being foolish enough to run with an ax in your hand? That's not very smart, but it's not exactly against the law."

Relief flooded the farmer's face. He bobbed his head and said, "Thank you, Marshal, thank you."

"Take care of your wife now, and when she feels a little better maybe you can give me a hand throwing these fellows over their saddles."

"Wh-what're you gonna do with 'em?"

"Take them to Burnt Creek, I suppose. That's the closest place I'll find an undertaker, isn't it?"

"Yeah, but it . . . it's Burnt Creek, Marshal. That's the last place you want to go right now. These fellas rode with Cal Rainey."

Tilghman's eyes narrowed. He knew something had been nagging at the back of his brain, and now he realized what it was. Earlier, the farmer had mentioned the name Rainey. Tilghman remembered where he had heard it before.

He asked, "Who's Cal Rainey?"

"He's the leader of the bunch that's been runnin' wild around here. Don't tell anybody I said that, though. They . . . they don't like folks talkin' about them."

"I thought the marshal in Burnt Creek was named Rainey."

"He is. Dave Rainey. And the mayor is Martin Rainey. They're Cal's brothers."

Well, thought Tilghman. The job that had brought him here had just gotten a mite more interesting . . . and challenging.

Chapter 4

It was late in the afternoon by the time Tilghman reached Burnt Creek, leading two horses with grisly burdens draped over their saddles and lashed down. The smell of blood made the animals skittish, but Tilghman kept a firm hand on the reins.

He wasn't surprised that his arrival drew a crowd. A stranger riding into town was enough to stir some interest in most frontier settlements. A stranger with a couple of dead men definitely made folks pay attention.

Several children started trotting alongside the horses, trying to get a closer look at the corpses. Tilghman glanced over his shoulder and said, "You kids get away from there."

"Did you kill 'em, mister?" a little boy called.

"They didn't give me any choice," Tilghman replied.

That was the way he handled himself as a lawman. He didn't draw his gun unless he had to, didn't shoot unless he had to, didn't shoot to kill unless there was no other way. When he was gone, he didn't want anybody ever saying that Bill Tilghman had been trigger-happy and kill-crazy.

But they wouldn't say that he had ever backed down from trouble, either.

Since the curious kids weren't leaving, Tilghman asked them, "Where can I find the marshal's office?"

A couple of the youngsters pointed to a squat stone building on the left side of the street, half a block ahead. Tilghman nodded, said, "Much obliged," and angled his mount in that direction.

The business section of Burnt Creek was laid out in a square, but instead of a courthouse in the middle there was a three-story frame building with the words DROVERS HOTEL painted in big letters on the side of it. Across the front was emblazoned the legend DROVERS SALOON. The place didn't make any secret who its clientele was.

The other businesses were the usual mix of saloons, restaurants, general mercantiles, hardware and farm implement stores, saddle shops, bootmakers, a dress shop and milliner's, a bank, a newspaper office, a couple of doctor's offices, three or four lawyers, a Chinese laundry, and an apothecary. The streets that formed the square extended outward to other cross-streets lined with residences. The stream that gave the settlement its name lay a quarter of a mile west of town.

Tilghman had seen dozens of town much like this one. They had sprung up all over Oklahoma Territory during the past few years, as more and more of the former Indian Territory was opened for settlement.

As he neared the marshal's office, he passed the big hotel and saloon in the center of the square and noticed a smaller sign on the wall next to the front door. MARTIN RAINEY, PROP., it read. Another of Cal Rainey's brothers and the mayor of Burnt Creek, Tilghman recalled the farmer saying. And Cal Rainey was the leader of the outlaws everyone feared.

Of course, that didn't mean that Dave and Martin Rainey were anything other than decent, law-abiding citizens. There had been plenty of cases where one member of a family had crossed the line and become an outlaw. Tilghman told himself to keep an open mind and give the other Rainey brothers the benefit of the doubt, unless and until they proved otherwise.

The marshal must have heard the commotion that Tilghman's arrival with the dead men had generated. He emerged from his office as Tilghman reined to a halt in front of the building. Dave Rainey was a stocky man with sandy hair receding from a high forehead. The black butt of a revolver stuck up from a cross-draw rig on his left hip. He cradled a shotgun in both hands, pointed down at the boardwalk but ready to tilt up and fire if necessary.

"That's far enough, mister," the marshal said.

"It's about as far as I intended to go," Tilghman said. "Got a couple of bodies here for the local undertaker, if you can point me to him or send somebody to fetch him."

Dave Rainey ignored that request and said, "Did you kill them?"

"I did. They shot first. They also threatened the lives of a farmer and his wife a good number of miles east of here."

"Who would that be?"

Tilghman said, "Huh. You know, I never did

get their names."

"So all I've got to go by about what happened is your word."

Tilghman stiffened in the saddle. He didn't care much for the challenging tone in the local badge-toter's voice. He said, "My word is good. And even if it's not, the sign on the building says you're the town marshal of Burnt Creek, so whatever happened it was a long way outside your jurisdiction."

"You brought the bodies into town. That makes it my business. And who are you to go talking about jurisdiction?"

Tilghman pushed his coat back to reveal his badge.

"Somebody whose bailiwick covers the whole territory. Deputy U.S. Marshal Bill Tilghman."

He could tell by the look in Dave Rainey's eyes that the man had heard of him. Rainey said gruffly, "Why the hell didn't you say so? The undertaking parlor is on the other side of the square. I'll send my deputy for him." He looked into the crowd that had gathered behind Tilghman. "Coley, go fetch Doc Graves."

A tall, skinny young man wearing a huge hat that threatened to swallow up his head said, "Sure, Marshal," and loped off.

"Your undertaker is named Graves?" Tilghman said.

"Yeah. Fitting, ain't it?"

"And he's a doctor, too?"

"Them he can't save, he plants. It's efficient, he says."

"You'd think folks would accuse him of trying to drum up business for his undertaking parlor," Tilghman said dryly.

"If he did that, then people wouldn't hire him as a doctor."

Tilghman shrugged and said, "I suppose that makes sense."

"Why don't you get down and tie those horses, Marshal? Nobody will bother them until Doc Graves gets here with his wagon. I've got a pot of coffee on the stove."

Tilghman hadn't had any coffee since breakfast, so that sounded good to him. He swung down from the saddle.

As he did so, another man came bustling along the boardwalk. He wore a brown suit and hat, was clean-shaven, and had a beefy, well-fed face. Tilghman glanced back and forth between the marshal and the newcomer and saw the resemblance between them. He knew he was looking at the other Rainey brother,

Martin, the mayor of Burnt Creek.

"What's going on here?" Martin Rainey demanded in an officious tone. "Are those men dead?"

"Never was able to put anything past you, Mart," Dave replied.

Martin's already florid face flushed a little darker.

"You shouldn't be talking to me like that," he said. "I'm your boss, you know, as well as your older brother."

"Yeah, sorry," Dave muttered, although he sounded to Tilghman like he didn't mean it. He nodded toward the federal lawman and went on, "This is Deputy U.S. Marshal Tilghman, who rode over here from Guthrie, I reckon."

"That's right," Tilghman said.

Martin Rainey's demeanor instantly became more deferential. He extended a hand and said, "Marshal Tilghman, it's an honor to meet you. I've heard a great deal about you. I'm Martin Rainey. Mayor Rainey, I should say." He shook hands, then hooked his thumbs in his vest in a preening manner. "Burnt Creek is my town, I suppose you could say."

Dave looked like he wanted to argue that, but instead he said, "The marshal and I were about to have some coffee. You want to join us, Mart?"

"Actually, I do. I want to hear about what brings such a distinguished law enforcement officer to our town."

The three men went into the office, which was sparsely furnished with a scarred old desk, a few ladderback chairs, a couple of cabinets, and a pot-bellied stove. Dave Rainey got tin cups from a drawer in the desk and poured coffee for them.

As he handed one of the cups to Tilghman, he asked, "Are you here on business, Marshal, or did you come to Burnt Creek because it was the closest place you could bring those bodies?"

Tilghman took a sip of the strong, black brew, then said, "Some of both. Marshal Nix in Guthrie sent me out here because of reports he's gotten about a bunch of rustlers and road agents causing trouble in these parts."

He didn't say anything about how the farmer had identified Cal Rainey as the leader of that gang. He would keep that card close to his vest for now.

Martin Rainey frowned and said, "I don't recall hearing anything about that, do you, Dave?"

With a shrug, Dave said, "The drovers who

bring their herds through here on the way to Colorado are always complaining about something. They claim they get cheated here in town, and they say they lose some stock when they come through here. I never figured it amounted to much. Some of the farmers might pick off a stray cow or two for beef for their families. It's hard making a go of it on these little homesteads."

"I was under the impression the losses were on a larger scale than that, and several men have been killed in the raids."

"I wouldn't know anything about that," Dave said blandly.

"What about the problems they've had here in town?"

"There haven't been any problems," Martin said. "You know how those cowboys are, Marshal. Most of them are from Texas, and they're a proddy bunch. They're never happy unless they're raising hell. Other than the sort of minor disturbances you find in all trail towns, things have been pretty peaceful here in Burnt Creek."

"I see," Tilghman said as he nodded slowly. "From the sound of it, Marshal Nix was misinformed, and so was I."

"That's the way it seems to me, too," Dave said.

But despite Tilghman's comment, he didn't believe for a second that the complaints Marshal Nix had received weren't legitimate. He had been a lawman long enough to recognize it when somebody tried to pull the wool over his eyes.

Every instinct in his body told him that the Rainey brothers were both as crooked as a dog's hind leg.

Chapter 5

After talking apparently idly with the marshal and the mayor for a few more minutes, Tilghman said, "I guess I'll start back to Guthrie tomorrow. I need to hunt up a livery stable for my horse and a hotel room for me."

"The Gonzalez Livery is less than a block off the square," Martin said, "and I can help you with the hotel room. I operate the Drovers Hotel. You must have seen it when you rode into town."

Tilghman put a smile on his face.

"I did," he agreed. "You've got a mighty fine-looking establishment, Mayor."

"I'm proud of it. Why don't you come along with me, and I'll see to it that you're fixed up properly? Dave, find Coley and have him take the marshal's horse down to the Mexican's barn."

"Sure," Dave said. "If there's anything else you need, Marshal, you just let one of us know and we'll see to it."

Still smiling, Tilghman said, "You boys sure know how to make a fella feel welcome."

"Least we can do for a fellow officer of the law."

Tilghman felt anger boil up inside him, but he kept it tamped down and concealed. If he was right about the Rainey brothers, he didn't have anything in common with either of them, and he didn't like Dave making it sound like he did.

But for the time being he would play along with them and see what else he could find out.

Tilghman and Martin Rainey crossed the street to the Drovers Saloon and Hotel. The building had an actual lawn around it, although the grass was short and starting to turn brown from the summer heat. There was also a wrap-around verandah, the roof of which formed a second-floor balcony. It must have cost quite a bit to have enough lumber freighted out here to build the three-story structure, thought Tilghman.

As they went inside, Martin explained that the dining room and saloon were on the first floor, flanking the lobby, guest rooms were on the second floor, and his private quarters took up the third floor.

In the lobby, Martin told the clerk on duty at the desk to give Tilghman the best room in the house, no charge.

"I appreciate it, but I can't do that, Mayor," Tilghman said as he shook his head. "Marshal Nix would frown on it. As long as I get a receipt for my expense account, that'll be fine."

"All right, if that's the way you want it," Martin said. "I know you federal marshals don't make much money."

"Six cents a mile while on official business," Tilghman said. "If a fella stays busy, he can make enough to keep himself together. Nobody's going to get rich packing a badge for Uncle Sam, though."

Martin pointed through an arched entrance to the left of the lobby and said, "The saloon is through there, if you want a drink. You'll let me buy the first round, won't you?"

"I would if I drank, which I don't."

"How about some supper, then?" Martin indicated another arched door on the other side of the lobby. "The hotel dining room is over there."

"I reckon that would be all right," Tilghman said. "I'm obliged to you."

He didn't want to be in Martin Rainey's debt at all, but it wouldn't pay for him to be too stiff-necked. He wanted folks to relax around him. That way they were more likely to let something slip that they weren't supposed to.

Tilghman signed the registration book, took a key from the clerk, and went upstairs carrying the saddlebags and Winchester he had picked up from his horse when he and Martin Rainey left the marshal's office. The Drovers Hotel wasn't exactly fancy, but it was fixed up pretty nice. Tilghman's room had a rug on the floor, and the bed looked comfortable.

He left his gear there and went back down to the dining room. He hadn't been seated at one of the tables for more than a minute when a nice-looking young blond woman in a print dress and a starched apron came up to the table and asked, "What can I get for you, Marshal Tilghman?"

He wasn't surprised that word of who he was had gotten around town. He placed his hat carefully on the table and asked, "What's good from the kitchen?"

The blonde didn't hesitate in answering, "I'd

order the pot roast. It's cooked with potatoes, carrots, and onions. Mrs. Harrigan adds a secret ingredient to it, too." She leaned closer and lowered her voice conspiratorially. "I guess it would be all right to tell you, though. It's a dash of sherry."

Even though Tilghman didn't drink, he didn't object to a little wine used in cooking. He smiled and nodded to the waitress.

"That sounds mighty good, all right. I'll have that and a pot of coffee. And maybe a slice of apple pie, if you've got it."

"We do. I'll be right back with the coffee."

While he was sitting there alone at the table, Tilghman looked around the dining room. It wasn't very busy, with only half a dozen customers besides him. He had seen from glancing at the registration book as he signed it and the key rack behind the desk that the hotel didn't have a lot of guests at the moment. If business was like this all the time, then Martin Rainey couldn't be making much money. Not enough to justify building such a big place.

The blond waitress came back with the coffee. As she poured it, Tilghman said, "Do you mind if I ask your name, miss?"

"Not at all, Marshal. It's Casey."

She smiled at him, bold as brass, and he couldn't help but notice the scattering of freckles across her nose and the dimple in her chin. He realized she was flirting with him despite the fact his saddle was probably as old as she was.

Tilghman's wife Flora was back on the ranch he owned, and even if she hadn't been, he wasn't in the habit of messing around with young women. It went against his moral beliefs.

But he wanted information from Casey, so he wasn't above returning her smile and making her think he enjoyed her company. In point of fact, he did enjoy it. Any man would. Casey was mighty pretty.

"Business been sort of slack here lately, Casey?"

Still holding the coffee pot, she frowned a little in thought as she propped her other hand on her hip.

"No, not really," she said. "No more so than usual. This is about as busy as it ever gets."

"What about when the herds come through?"

"Oh, things get pretty hectic in the saloon then, I suppose, but I don't work over there on that side so I don't know for sure. I just know it's noisier during those times. But the cowboys all spend the night where they camp with the herd, they don't stay here."

Tilghman nodded. That was pretty much what he'd figured. If a man moved into a new town, built a big hotel, and then saw it losing money, he might be more likely to turn to some other endeavor to make money.

Like putting together a gang of rustlers with his brothers.

That was sheer speculation at this point, however. Tilghman trusted his instincts, but he also warned himself about jumping to conclusions. He needed to dig around more and see where the trail took him.

Casey was right about the pot roast being good. Tilghman was comfortably full when he left the hotel after the meal. He had asked Casey for directions to Gonzalez's Livery Stable. That was where he turned his footsteps.

It was a nice evening. The warmth of the day had already begun to ease, leaving just a hint of coolness in the breeze stirred across the Oklahoma prairie. A hint of red from the departed sun lingered in the western sky. Tilghman breathed deeply of the air and felt that life was basically good, despite the fact he was here to deal with a gang of thieves and killers.

He heard a man singing softly in Spanish as he walked into the barn, which was located at the end of the block away from the square. Tilghman followed the song to an empty stall, where a stocky, dark-haired man in overalls forked hay from a bin. He rested the pitchfork's handle on the hard-packed ground and asked, "What can I do for you, señor?"

"You've already done it," Tilghman said. He pointed to the next stall and went on, "That's my horse, and from the looks of things, you're taking fine care of him."

A smile stretched across the man's face.

"Oh, you are the Marshal Tilghman," he said. "Coley Barnett said this horse, he belong to you."

"You're Señor Gonzalez?"

"Sí, Raoul Gonzalez." He wiped his hand on his overalls and extended it. "It is an honor, Marshal."

Tilghman shook with him.

"The whole town is talking about you and the dead men you brought in," Gonzalez continued. "Some say they were part of the gang that has moved in these past few months."

"You know about that gang, do you?"

"Sí, but of course. I am also the blacksmith,

and when the herds come through, usually several of the vaqueros with them need me to tighten a horseshoe or replace one for them. I hear talk about how the rustlers have caused trouble for them."

So the liveryman knew about the rustling, but the marshal and the mayor claimed they hadn't heard anything about it. That was one more bit of evidence to support Tilghman's hunch that Dave and Martin were in on the lawbreaking with their brother Cal.

"You know a man named Cal Rainey?"

A lantern hung on a nail next to the door of Gonzalez's office, just inside the open double doors of the barn. The yellow glow it cast wasn't very bright, but it was enough for Tilghman to see the worried look that suddenly passed over Gonzalez's face.

"Sí, Señor Cal Rainey owns a ranch five miles north of here. He doesn't come to town very often."

"Even though his brothers both live here?"

Gonzalez jerked his shoulders in a shrug.

"That is their business, not mine, señor marshal."

"Sure," Tilghman said easily. "Didn't mean to gossip. Mostly I just wanted to check on my horse, and I can see he's just fine."

"I will have him ready for you early in the morning, so you can start back to Guthrie."

So word had gotten around he was leaving. Tilghman supposed Martin and Dave Rainey were responsible for that.

He told Gonzalez buenos noches, then left to head back to the hotel. The last of the daylight had faded from the sky, leaving night to settle down over Burnt Creek.

He was almost back to the square when boot leather scraped on the ground behind him. The sound wasn't loud, but it was enough to warn him, especially since he had just passed the dark mouth of a narrow passage between buildings. Tilghman swung around.

Twin gouts of flame exploded from the muzzles of a shotgun less than ten feet away.

Chapter 6

Tilghman was already moving, diving forward onto the ground. The shotgun's deafening blast slammed painfully against his ears, but that was the only thing to hit him. The double load of buckshot hadn't had time to spread out much. All the deadly pellets flew over him, spraying the boardwalk and the fronts of the buildings along the street.

The bushwhacker had made a crucial mistake by firing both barrels at once. If he had fired – and missed – with only one, he could have tilted the weapon down and finished off Tilghman with the second barrel, then and there.

As it was, the man didn't have time to reload and could only use the shotgun as a club as Tilghman pushed himself up and drove forward to tackle him around the knees. The shotgun barrels struck Tilghman a painful blow in the back, but he ignored it and heaved, upending his attacker. The man went over backward with a startled yell.

Tilghman scrambled after him and hammered his clenched fist against the man's chest. The bushwhacker had managed to hang on to the shotgun. He struck desperately with it. The stock clipped Tilghman on the jaw and knocked him away. Tilghman rolled over and clawed the Colt from its holster.

His attacker had made it to his feet. Tilghman didn't want to give the man time to reload, so he angled the .45's barrel up and fired. It was too dark for him to see if he had hit his target.

Evidently not, because the next second he caught a glimpse of the bushwhacker running away, silhouetted momentarily against the glow coming through the still open doors of Raoul Gonzalez's livery barn. Lying on his belly, Tilghman gripped his right wrist with his left hand to steady it, drew a bead, and fired again.

Even in that bad light, he might have hit the bushwhacker if the fleeing man hadn't chosen that exact instant to dart around a corner. If

Tilghman had been the sort to indulge in profanity, he would have cussed his bad luck. He could get up and give chase, but the hombre would have time now to pause and slip a couple of fresh shells into the shotgun. Charging after a loaded scattergun in the dark was a mighty efficient way for a man to get himself killed, thought Tilghman.

Besides, somebody else was coming. He heard the rapid footsteps approaching behind him.

Tilghman rolled to the side and sat up. The Colt was level in his hand as he called, "Hold it right there."

The footsteps stopped. A familiar voice said, "Marshal Tilghman? Is that you?"

There was a hitch rack close by Tilghman's left shoulder. He reached up, caught hold of it, and steadied himself as he climbed to his feet.

"Yeah, it's me," he said.

"I heard shots," Marshal Dave Rainey said. "Are you hit?"

"No, I'm fine." He would have some bruises in the morning, but those didn't count.

"What happened?"

"Somebody cut down on me with a double-barrel. I threw a couple of bullets back at him, but he got away."

"He shot at you with both barrels and you weren't hit? How in the world did you manage that?"

"Just lucky, I guess," Tilghman said dryly. Working easily by feel, he ejected the two spent shells from his Colt and thumbed in fresh rounds to take their place.

Rainey came close enough for Tilghman to see him better. The local lawman was carrying a shotgun, but Tilghman knew Dave wasn't the one who had ambushed him. Rainey hadn't had time to circle around and get behind him, and also even the brief glimpse Tilghman had gotten of his attacker was enough to tell him that the man had been taller and slimmer than Dave Rainey.

Some of the citizens of Burnt Creek were coming along the street now, drawn by the sound of gunfire and wanting to know what had happened. Rainey turned and confronted them, telling them that there was nothing to see here and ordering them to go on about their business. As the crowd began to disperse before it ever really had a chance to form, Rainey swung back around to Tilghman and said, "Come on over to the office with me. I want to hear more about what happened."

Tilghman pouched his iron. He had a hunch that even though the local marshal hadn't pulled the trigger, he knew something about the ambush attempt. Tilghman would play along for the moment, but he wouldn't let down his guard.

They walked up the street to the marshal's office and found Martin Rainey waiting for them in front of the building.

"I heard shots," the mayor said with a worried frown on his beefy face.

His brother grunted and said, "I reckon everybody in town did. Sounded like a war for a second there." Dave nodded toward Tilghman. "Somebody tried to ventilate the marshal."

"How terrible! I hope you don't think such things happen all the time in Burnt Creek, Marshal Tilghman. I'd like to believe that we're more civilized than that."

"No, I figure this was a special case," Tilghman said. "Whoever it was, he was after me, probably because I came to look into the rustling that's been going on."

"I thought we'd established that rustling isn't that big a problem around here," Martin said with a frown.

"Maybe not. But if that's true, why would somebody try to blow a hole in me?"

Tilghman saw the glance that passed between the brothers. He had them thinking that they had overplayed their hand and aroused his suspicions, when in truth he had never been convinced by the game they were playing. But if there was a chance he might cause dissension in the ranks of his enemies, he wasn't going to pass up the opportunity.

Dave grunted and said, "Come on inside and we'll talk about it."

"Actually, Marshal, I've decided that I'm pretty tired," Tilghman said. "And there's not much to say besides what I've already told you. I think I'll just go on over to the hotel and get some rest, if that's all right."

"Why, sure, whatever you want," Dave said. "If you have any more problems, let me know."

Martin said sharply, "I'm sure Marshal Tilghman won't have the same sort of problem again. Whoever shot at him, the man is long gone now and I doubt if he'll come back."

Tilghman said, "Hope you're right, Mayor," and turned away to hide the grin that briefly stretched across his face. From the sound of it, bushwhacking him had been Dave's idea, and

Martin wasn't any too happy about it.

He walked across the street to the hotel and left the brothers behind him to go into the marshal's office and wrangle over what they ought to do next.

One thing he was reasonably sure of: whatever they decided wouldn't be good for him and his investigation. They couldn't afford to leave him alone and let him continue with the job that had brought him here.

He had already stirred up trouble just by being here. Starting tomorrow he would poke the hive a little harder and see how many bees came flying out.

He would have to be careful, though. Some of these bees had double-barreled stingers.

The clerk behind the desk in the lobby gave him a friendly nod when he came in.

"Evening, Marshal Tilghman," the man said. "How are you enjoying your stay in Burnt Creek so far?"

"Fine and dandy," Tilghman said, and it would have taken a keen ear to hear the underlying tone of dry humor in his words. He got his room key from the man and headed upstairs.

Before leaving earlier, he had taken the

precaution of wedging a tiny piece of broken matchstick into the gap between the door of his room and the jamb. Nobody would notice it if they weren't looking for it, especially in the relatively dim light of the corridor.

As he came up to the door, though, Tilghman saw that the telltale bit of wood was missing. Somebody had gone into his room while he was out.

Whoever it was might even still be in there.

Since he had already encountered somebody wielding a shotgun earlier tonight, he was acutely aware of how much damage such a weapon could do. At close range, it could fire a load of buckshot through the thin panels of the door.

So when he inserted the key into the lock and turned it with a metallic rattle, he had it in his outstretched left arm and was standing well to the right of the door itself. His other hand rested on the butt of the Colt on his hip.

No shots blasted from inside the room. That wasn't enough to convince Tilghman nobody was in there waiting to ambush him again. He threw the door open and went in low and fast, gun in hand now and tracking from side to side, ready to erupt with smoke, flame, and lead.

He noticed that somebody had lit the lamp on the little table beside the bed. Just as his senses registered that, he heard a frightened gasp from his right and swung in that direction. His finger was taut on the trigger, needing only the least bit more pressure for the gun to fire.

Tilghman stopped squeezing the trigger just in time. He stared in surprise over the Colt's barrel at a face lightly dusted with freckles. Big blue eyes stared back at him in fright.

"Casey!" Tilghman exclaimed in disgust. He was a little shaken, too, by the knowledge of just how close he had come to shooting her. "What in blue blazes are you doing here?"

For a second she seemed to be still too scared to speak. Then she swallowed hard and forced out an answer.

"I want to help you," she said. "I want to help you round up Cal Rainey and his gang."

Chapter 7

Well, that was a relief, anyway, thought Tilghman. When he'd first seen the uninvited visitor in his room and realized who she was, he had thought for an instant she had something unsavory in mind. That would have been flattering in a way, but not anything Tilghman would have cared to explore.

But as far as her helping him carry out his assignment . . . that he was interested in.

He lowered the Colt and slipped it back in its holster as he eased the door closed behind him.

"Or would you rather I left it open?" he asked, lifting one eyebrow.

Casey smiled.

"I think I trust you not to do anything improper, Marshal Tilghman," she said. "You're known for your high moral standards . . . as well as for being hell on lawbreakers."

Despite the smile on her face, he saw worry lurking in her eyes. Something was bothering her bad enough to make her sneak up here and let herself into his room. He assumed that since she worked in the hotel, she wouldn't have a lot of trouble getting her hands on a key that let her into the rooms.

He took off his hat and tossed it on the bed.

"Why don't you tell me exactly what it is that brings you here?" he suggested.

"You're after Cal Rainey's bunch, aren't you?"

"I'm after whoever is responsible for the rustling and general thievery that's been going on around here."

"That's Cal Rainey," Casey said.

"His brothers claim there's not really a rustling problem."

Casey rolled her blue eyes and asked, "What do you expect them to say? They're Cal's brothers. Besides . . . " She lowered her voice. "You didn't hear it from me, but I wouldn't be surprised if Marshal Rainey and the mayor know a lot more about what Cal's been doing than they're letting on."

That was exactly what Tilghman thought too, but he didn't mention that to Casey. Instead, he pulled another chair over and told her, "Have a seat, Miss . . . I'm afraid I don't know your last name."

"It's Spencer. Casey Spencer." She sat down and folded her hands in her lap rather primly.

Tilghman turned the other chair around and straddled it. He said, "What's your connection with Cal Rainey's gang?"

"What makes you think I'm connected with them?"

"You seem to know what they've been up to," Tilghman replied with a shrug. "And you've got to have a good reason for wanting me to bring them to justice."

"You mean besides it being the right thing to do?"

"I don't doubt that folks sometimes do things just because they're right. But it's a lot easier if taking action benefits them in some way, too."

The worry broke free in Casey's eyes then, in the form of tears that reflected the lamplight. She blinked them back, dabbed at her eyes with the back of a hand, and said, "It's a boy. A young man, really. A . . . a friend of mine."

"Maybe a little more than a friend?"

"We talked about getting married. But he said we couldn't do it on a cowhand's wages, and he insisted no wife of his was going to work in a hotel. Then he quit his riding job, and the last few times he's come around, he's had money. I can only think of one way he might've gotten it."

"What's this young fella's name?"

"Boone Scanlon."

"You realize that if I break up the gang and arrest them, Boone's liable to wind up behind bars, too."

Casey's chin lifted a little. She said, "I know. That's better than him winding up as a hardened criminal, being a fugitive all his life, and finally being shot or hanged at a young age. He's basically a good man, Marshal. I know he can't have done anything too terrible so far. If . . . if he's sent to prison for a few years, that'll be bad, but he can serve his time and when he gets out, the two of us can make a fresh start somewhere."

Tilghman thought a couple of things were wrong with her way of looking at the situation. For one, if she was right about Boone Scanlon being part of Cal Rainey's gang, she had no way of knowing just how bad he was. He might have committed crimes already that would put a hangman's noose around his neck. For another, even if her belief in Scanlon's basic goodness was justified, once he was an ex-convict they would have a lot harder time starting over than she supposed.

But hope came naturally to the young, he reminded himself, and on rare occasions things even worked out the way folks wanted them to.

Anyway, his job was to put an end to the lawlessness in the area, by whatever means were necessary. If that meant crushing the dreams of a young woman, he supposed he could do it.

Didn't mean he had to like it, though.

"All right," he said. "Tell me everything you know. I can't make any promises where your friend's concerned, though."

"I understand. Just . . . if there's any way you can help him . . . "

"I'll do what I can," Tilghman said, then grimaced slightly as he realized he had just made a promise after telling her he couldn't.

"Thank you," Casey said. "Boone used to ride for a rancher named Driscoll. Then a friend of his quit and went to work for Cal Rainey on the Boxed CR spread. It's not much of a ranch, but Rainey and the men who work for him always seem to have plenty of money."

Tilghman nodded. That was pretty suspicious, all right, but it wasn't evidence.

"I think Boone got it in his head that he could make some fast money by working for Rainey, too, so he drew his time from Mr. Driscoll about a month ago. Since then I've only seen him a few times, but he seemed . . . different."

"Different how?"

"Harder. Like he didn't care about people anymore. Except for me. He was still nice to me. He told me it wouldn't be long before we could get married, but that we'd have to leave Burnt Creek when we did. He didn't want to stay around these parts anymore."

Tilghman could understand that. Scanlon must be afraid that his connection to the rustlers would come to light if he tried to stay around Burnt Creek.

"When was the last time you saw him?"

"It's been about a week," Casey said.

"Did he drop any hints about what the gang was planning to do next?"

If Tilghman could catch them in the act of committing a crime, it would make his job a little easier. He would have justification then for any actions he might have to take.

"No, not really, but like I said, he told me it wouldn't be long. That means they're about to do something else illegal, doesn't it?"

"More than likely," Tilghman agreed.

"I wish you could stop them before . . . before things get even worse for Boone."

"I need more to go on than that," he told her. "Can you remember anything at all he might have said? Anything that seemed suspicious or not like him?"

Casey frowned as she obviously thought hard, trying to remember everything Scanlon had said to her. The frown didn't make her any less pretty.

Finally, after a long moment, she said, "He mentioned something about the Devil's Hand."

The name struck a very faint chord in Tilghman's memory, but he couldn't come up with what it meant.

"What's the Devil's Hand?" he asked.

"It's a rock formation northwest of here in the Gypsum Hills. Actually, it's a series of ridges, shaped and arranged like the fingers of a man's hand if they were splayed out a little. But because they're so rugged and gnarled, people started calling the whole area the Devil's Hand."

Tilghman remembered hearing about the

place now. He had never been there, but it was supposed to be a pretty inhospitable area, not much better than badlands.

"Is that part of Cal Rainey's range?"

"I don't think it belongs to anybody," Casey said. "It's not really good for farming or ranching, although I suppose you could graze some cattle on it. The ridges are mostly rock, but there's a little grass between them. That's what I've heard people say, anyway. I've never actually been there."

Tilghman's keen mind worked quickly. From the sound of it, there was nothing in the Devil's Hand for Cal Rainey and his gang to rob . . . but they might be putting it to a different purpose. He had figured they were selling off the rustled stock as they stole it, but it was possible they had been gathering the cattle into a bigger herd, one that would net them a larger payoff from the beef dealers when they finally drove the herd north into Kansas. If that was the case, they would need a place to keep all those stolen cattle . . .

And the Devil's Hand might work just fine as a temporary refuge.

Tilghman's pulse quickened. If such a herd really was there and he could tie it to Cal

Rainey, it wouldn't just serve as proof of Rainey's guilt. He might be able to recover the rustled stock as well and return the cows to their rightful owners. He would have to call in help to handle that, but it could be done.

That would be a good way to wrap up the assignment. Marshal Nix couldn't ask for any better results. The first step, Tilghman told himself, was to check out the Devil's Hand and make sure those cows were there.

Those thoughts flashed through Tilghman's mind in a matter of seconds. He nodded and told Casey, "I'll look into it."

"Thank you. And if there's any way to help Boone . . . "

"We'll see," Tilghman said, keeping his response vague. He stood up, moved over to the door, and went on, "You'd better be going now, but before you do, let me take a gander outside to make sure nobody's in the hall."

"You don't want anyone to see me leaving your room."

"I reckon it'd be better that way. Neither of us need the gossip. We both have jobs to do."

He opened the door a few inches, checked the hallway as best he could, and when he didn't see anyone, he pulled the door back more and stuck his head out. The corridor was empty all the way up and down.

He stepped back and motioned for Casey to leave. She moved to do so, but she paused just before stepping through the door. Taking Tilghman by surprise, she raised herself on her toes and kissed his cheek, brushing her lips across his leathery skin.

"Thank you, Marshal," she whispered.

"Save your thanks until I've actually done something."

"I know you'll help Boone. I have confidence in you."

Tilghman didn't say anything else as Casey hurried soft-footed toward the landing, but he was confident, too. Confident that he would do his job.

Even if it meant putting Boone Scanlon's neck in a noose and breaking Casey Spencer's heart.

Chapter 8

The attempt on his life was enough to make Tilghman even more careful than usual. He propped a chair under the doorknob, heaped up the covers in the middle of the bed with a couple of pillows under them to make it look like he was sleeping there, and stretched out on the floor on the far side of the bed instead, with his Colt and Winchester right beside him. It wasn't the most comfortable place in the world to sleep, but he had spent nights in worse situations.

His precautions weren't really needed. Nothing happened except that he was a little stiff the next morning. He pulled on his clothes and went downstairs with a plan in mind, the first step of which was to get a good breakfast and a pot of coffee inside him.

Casey was working in the dining room. She gave him a brief, perfunctory smile as he came in and sat down. No one would have been able to tell by looking at her that she had been in his room the night before. She came over to him and said, "Good morning, Marshal. Do you want coffee?"

"Yes, ma'am," he told her. "And a big plate of whatever you've got in the kitchen for breakfast."

"Ham, eggs, and biscuits."

"Sounds good to me."

She brought the coffee, and while Tilghman was sipping his first cup, Marshal Dave Rainey came into the dining room and looked around. Tilghman figured Rainey was looking for him, and sure enough, the local lawman spotted him and came straight across the room toward his table.

"Any more trouble last night, Marshal?" Rainey asked.

"Not a bit," Tilghman replied. He nodded toward the empty chair on the other side of the table. "Care to join me?"

"Don't mind if I do," Rainey said as he took off his hat and pulled out the chair.

Tilghman caught Casey's eye and signaled for

her to bring another cup.

"You're starting back to Guthrie today?" Rainey asked.

"I'll be riding out in a little while, after I've had my breakfast," Tilghman said.

That wasn't a lie. He would be leaving Burnt Creek, all right. But he wasn't heading for the territorial capital, although he intended to start in that direction. Once he was out of sight of the settlement, he would swing around, skirt it well to the north, and ride for the Devil's Hand.

Casey brought the extra cup, poured coffee for Rainey, and asked, "Will you be having breakfast as well, Marshal?"

"No, thanks, I already ate," he told her. "Just the coffee will be fine."

"All right." She smiled at Tilghman, again just an expression of professional politeness, and told him, "Your food will be out soon, Marshal."

After she was gone, Rainey commented, "Pretty girl."

"I suppose. I'm a married man."

"Didn't strike you blind when you said 'I do', did it?" Rainey asked with a grin.

"Not hardly," Tilghman agreed dryly. "I don't reckon you were able to find out any more about that fella who tried to kill me last night."

Rainey's expression grew sober as he shrugged and said, "I asked around in some of the saloons. Nobody wanted to admit to knowing anything about it. Once it was light this morning I went down that alley where you said the bushwhacker ran off, looking for tracks. Thought he might have had a horse tied behind the building or something like that. But there weren't any hoofprints, and too many people had walked along there for any footprints to mean anything. I don't think an Apache could've trailed that fella with the shotgun. Sorry, Marshal."

That was just the sort of answer Tilghman had been expecting from Rainey.

"No need to be sorry," he said. "It sounds like you did everything you could. Anyway, I'll be out of here soon, and it won't be your worry anymore."

"I could ride with you for a ways," Rainey suggested. "Just to make sure nobody tries anything else."

Casey came out of the kitchen carrying a tray of food. Tilghman saw her coming and told Rainey, "That won't be necessary. I'll be careful."

"Suit yourself. Just keep your eyes open."

Tilghman took another sip of his coffee, nodded, and said, "I always do."

Rainey got up and left as Tilghman dug into the food. When he was finished with breakfast, he left a half-dollar on the table for Casey and walked out of the dining room without looking at her. He went upstairs to get his rifle and gear from his room so that it would look like he was really checking out of the hotel and leaving town.

When Tilghman reached the livery stable, Raoul Gonzalez had his horse saddled and ready to ride.

"This is a fine mount you have, Señor Marshal Tilghman," the liveryman said as he patted the animal on the shoulder. "Thank you for entrusting me with his care."

Tilghman handed Gonzalez a five-dollar gold piece. He took the reins, then paused and asked, "Do you know an area called the Devil's Hand?"

A worried frown creased Gonzalez's forehead.

"Why do you want to know about that place?" he asked. "It is no good to anybody. And even worse . . . there is talk that it is haunted by evil spirits."

That revelation took Tilghman by surprise, which wasn't easy to do.

"Haunted?" he repeated. "Why in the world would anybody think that?"

"It is said that strange lights appear there at times, in the dark of the night, and there is a rumble of thunder even though the sky is completely clear overhead!"

"Well, that does sound a little unusual," Tilghman admitted. "How did you come to hear about this?"

"My cousin, he keeps a herd of sheep on the prairie at the edge of the Gypsum Hills. But he has grown frightened and now looks for another place to graze his sheep. You are not going out there, are you, Señor Marshal?"

"I'm on my way back to Guthrie," Tilghman said. "I just heard somebody talking about the Devil's Hand and was curious."

Gonzalez made the sign of the cross and said, "Best not to be curious about evil places, my friend. They can lure you in . . . and never let you out!"

Tilghman wasn't worried about that. He had never seen a place he could get into that he couldn't get out of. But he didn't explain that to Gonzalez, just swung up into the saddle, waved farewell, and rode out of Burnt Creek heading east.

He felt eyes on him as he left and without appearing to do so, he flicked a glance at the hotel as he rode past. A curtain on a third-floor window twitched. Tilghman couldn't help but wonder if that was Mayor Martin Rainey's room.

He left the settlement behind him. It wouldn't have surprised him if Dave Rainey followed him, just to make sure he was going where he said he was. Tilghman didn't see anybody on his back trail when he looked behind him, though.

To be certain, he rode about three miles, then reined in as soon as he topped a small rise. He dismounted quickly, took a telescope from his saddlebags, and hurried back to the top of the slope, taking off his hat and dropping to hands and knees before he got there.

Tilghman bellied down in the grass and raised up just enough to scan the countryside behind him with the spyglass. He searched for any sign of someone trailing him but didn't see anything like that. The only things moving were birds soaring through the morning sky and a family of prairie dogs hunting for food. Tilghman grunted and closed the telescope.

The Rainey brothers thought he had given up

and was going home, just because they told him there wasn't a rustling problem in these parts. It was sort of annoying that they believed they could fool him so easily.

Tilghman wasn't going to turn down good luck, though, anywhere he found it.

Satisfied that he wasn't being followed, he got back onto his horse and began working his way north. Gradually, he swung around to the west. On this vast, mostly featureless grassland, it was difficult to judge distances, but eventually, a little past midday, he came in sight of some low, flat-topped hills and ridges on the western horizon.

Those were the Gypsum Hills, he knew, so called because of the layer of gypsum that crowned each of those flat tops, sparkling like glass in the sun.

Tilghman stopped at a creek to let his horse drink and rest a little. He always carried jerky in his saddlebags, so a couple of strips of the tough, savory stuff served as his lunch. Tilghman was of the old breed, much like the Indians, who could ride all day if he had to and survive on water and jerky.

While he was halted he checked his back trail again, out of habit, and still didn't see any pursuit.

Tilghman pushed on. It was late in the afternoon before he reached the hills. He didn't know exactly where the region known as the Devil's Hand was located. He would just have to search until he found it.

That search might extend well into the next day. This range of hills was pretty wide and ran far north, all the way to Kansas.

He didn't think he would have to go anywhere near that far, however. If the rustlers were using the Devil's Hand as their stronghold, it had to be somewhere reasonably close to Burnt Creek, which was half a day's ride to the southeast from where Tilghman was now.

He spent the rest of the day casting back and forth through the hills and along the shallow valleys that twisted between them. As Casey had told him, this range wouldn't be good for much of anything. It was too rugged and rocky for farming, and although some hardy grass grew in the valleys, it wasn't sufficient to provide permanent grazing for cattle.

There was enough that the area could be used as a temporary holding ground for a herd, though. Now that he had laid eyes on the place, Tilghman still believed that was a reasonable theory.

His search didn't yield any results, and as night quickly approached, he found a place to camp. A spring bubbled out of some rocks at the base of one of the hills, forming a tiny pool where his horse could drink. Tilghman would have enjoyed some coffee, but he decided not to build a fire. He could put up with a cold camp for one night, rather than risking being spotted.

He picketed his horse where the animal could graze on the scrubby grass, then after a meager supper of more jerky washed down with water from the spring, he spread his bedroll on the least rocky stretch of ground he could find and stretched out.

Tilghman had the true frontiersman's ability to sleep whenever and wherever he could, but he didn't doze off right away. Instead he thought about his home and his wife Flora. She was a good woman and seldom complained, but he knew she would have liked it if he gave up packing a badge and was content to stay home on their ranch.

He had tried to live that sort of settled life, he truly had, but something inside him made that difficult, if not impossible, for him to do. When he stayed too long in one place, he began to yearn for the feel of a saddle underneath him and the wind in his face. Some men just had to stay on the move, to be out and about, doing things, and Bill Tilghman was one of them.

He still hadn't gone to sleep when he heard what sounded like thunder. He was lying on his back, so he could see the whole sweep of the sky above him, and no clouds obscured the millions of stars in that vaulting black arch. That couldn't be thunder, Tilghman thought as he sat up and instinctively reached for the rifle beside him.

And then suddenly he knew what was making that sound.

Hooves. Thousands of hooves.

Somewhere not too far away, somebody was moving a herd of cattle in the night.

Chapter 9

Tilghman had his hat and boots on and was in the saddle in a hurry, not wanting to waste this chance. He followed the rumble of hooves, and as he came closer, he heard cattle bawling as well and even the click of horns against horns as close-packed animals jockeyed for position.

The moon hadn't risen yet, so he had only starlight to show him the way. The hills cast ebony shadows as he wound among them.

This was like a gunfight in a way. He couldn't afford to waste any time, but if he rushed, he ran the risk of his horse stumbling over something in the dark, falling, and breaking a leg. If that happened and he was set a-foot, it would ruin everything and might even cost him his life.

So he had to be careful and hope the cattle would be on the move long enough for him to catch up to them.

It wasn't long before Tilghman was able to sniff the air and smell the dust raised by that multitude of hooves. That told him he was closing in.

He reined to a stop beside one of the flat-topped ridges. He swung down from the saddle and dropped the reins, knowing the well-trained horse wouldn't wander off. With the Winchester gripped in his hand, Tilghman climbed the slope, which wasn't so steep that he couldn't manage by putting a hand down now and then to balance himself. He was careful not to step on rocks that might roll or slide under his feet and cause him to fall.

When he reached the crest, he saw that the ridge was about fifty yards wide. From the sound of it, the herd was right on the other side. Crouching as low as he could and still stay on his feet, so that he wouldn't be silhouetted against the stars, Tilghman ran across the mesa-like ridge top.

As he neared the edge he dropped to his knees and crawled forward. The rumble of hoofbeats and the bawling of cattle were loud now. He could see how someone might mistake the sounds for thunder. He had done so himself for a second when he first heard them.

Edging forward, Tilghman looked into the valley on the far side of the ridge. The herd was a dark mass stretching all the way to another ridge that was probably part of the formation known as the Devil's Hand. The dust rising from their hooves formed a gauzy veil in the sky that dimmed without completely obscuring the stars.

A man shouted somewhere close by. Tilghman looked down the slope to see a rider moving along the edge of the herd. His hands tightened on the rifle as he thought for a second that he had been spotted.

Then he saw the rider was trying to catch up to another man on horseback who reined in and turned back slightly to meet the one who had hailed him. They sat there for a moment on their horses, talking. The first man Tilghman had spotted waved an arm and pointed, like he was giving orders. The other one hauled his horse around and rode off quickly.

The first man stayed where he was. After a few seconds, the flare of a match told Tilghman the man had rolled a quirly. He set fire to the gasper, inhaling to get it going. The glare from the match flame revealed a hard-planed face, although Tilghman couldn't really make out many details.

From where he was, he could have shot the man out of the saddle. It was possible that the gunshot wouldn't be noticed because of all the noise the cattle were making.

But Tilghman was a lawman, not a cold-blooded killer.

Besides, the rustler would be a lot more helpful if Tilghman could take him alive.

The man hooked a leg around his saddle horn as he smoked. From the looks of that, he intended to stay here for a while and let the herd move on to wherever it was going.

Tilghman figured the outlaws had to move the cattle fairly often because the grazing was so poor in this area. Once they had eaten all the grass in one of these isolated valleys, they would have to be driven to another one.

Now that he knew where the rustlers were holed up, he could come back later with a posse and clean them out. For now he wanted to get his hands on Cal Rainey, the gang's ringleader. If he could force Cal to talk and admit that his brothers were part of the gang, too, Tilghman could arrest all three of them and take them back to Guthrie. The rest of the outlaws probably wouldn't be that dangerous without their leaders.

That was Tilghman's plan, anyway. He put it into motion by sliding over the edge of the hilltop and descending carefully toward the man who sat there on his horse, smoking.

While the noise of the cattle might not have been enough to mask a gunshot, it concealed any small sounds Tilghman made as he approached the rider. He was almost close enough to throw down on the man and order him to dismount when something went wrong. Some instinct must have warned the rustler. With the quirly still dangling from his lips, he yanked his horse around, grated a curse, and reached for the gun on his hip.

Tilghman lunged forward and swung the Winchester like a club. The barrel smashed into the man's right shoulder and drove him to one side on the horse's back. Tilghman dropped the rifle, grabbed the man's leg, and heaved, toppling him out of the saddle. As the man crashed to the ground, Tilghman drew his Colt and slapped the horse on the rump with his other hand, causing it to leap out of the way.

He hoped that the fall had stunned the rustler, but that wasn't the case. The man kicked up from the ground, the toe of his boot striking Tilghman's wrist and sending the Colt flying. Tilghman didn't have time to retrieve the Winchester. The rustler was already clawing out his own revolver.

Tilghman dived forward and landed on top of the man. He clamped his left hand around the wrist of the rustler's gun hand and drove his right fist into the man's face. It was a good, solid punch, but it wasn't enough to knock the man out. He bucked up from the ground and threw Tilghman to the side. They wound up rolling over and over as they wrestled for control of the rustler's gun.

Tilghman wound up on the bottom. His opponent drove a knee at his groin. Tilghman twisted to the side to take the vicious blow on his thigh. It hurt, but it wasn't incapacitating as it would have been if it had landed on its target.

Tilghman's fingers were like bands of iron around the other man's wrist. He knew that if he ever allowed the rustler to bring the gun into line, the roar of a shot at point-blank range would be the last thing he ever heard.

He hooked a punch into the man's

midsection, jerked his head aside to dodge a blow aimed at his face. His right hand shot straight up and closed around thc rustlcr's throat. The man hadn't yelled for help yet, and Tilghman didn't want him getting the chance to do so. With his grip on the man's throat, he forced the rustler to the side. Tilghman couldn't afford a shout or a shot, because he didn't know how close any of the other rustlers might be.

The two of them were evenly matched, both lean but with pantherish strength. A lucky break might well decide this fight. That break seemed to have come when the rustler snatched up a rock a little bigger than a man's fist and tried to bash Tilghman's brains out with it.

Tilghman twisted aside just in time to avoid the deadly blow. The rock smashed into the ground beside his head. Thrown off balance by the miss, the rustler wasn't able to brace himself when Tilghman suddenly jerked him closer. Tilghman lowered his head and drove the top of it into the man's face with smashing force. Blood spurted as the rustler's nose flattened under the impact. He went limp, stunned for the moment, anyway.

Tilghman wrenched the gun away from the

man and slapped it hard against the side of his head. That knocked him cold. Tilghman shoved him aside and climbed out from under him.

There was no time to waste. He used the man's own bandanna to tie his hands, then ripped a piece of cloth from the man's shirt and shoved it into his mouth to serve as a gag.

Quickly, Tilghman found his Colt and holstered it. He tucked the rustler's gun behind his belt.

The man's horse hadn't gone far. Tilghman approached it carefully, one hand extended, speaking in a soothing tone. The horse was skittish and danced around a little, but after a moment it allowed him to get close enough to grab the reins. Tilghman led it back over to the unconscious rustler.

Grunting with the effort, he hoisted the man across the back of the horse. A coiled lariat hung on the saddle. Tilghman used it to lash the rustler into place. Then he led the horse back around the ridge to where he had left his own mount.

A short time later, Tilghman rode away from the place, leading his captive's horse. He wasn't sure he could find the spot where he had camped earlier, but that didn't matter. He just wanted to put some distance between himself and the rest of the gang, along with his prisoner.

When he finally stopped, he couldn't hear the noise of the herd moving anymore. Either the cattle had moved on out of earshot, or else they had stopped as well after reaching their new temporary bedground.

The captured rustler had regained consciousness during the ride. He was making angry, muffled noises through the gag and squirming a little in his awkward position draped over the horse's back, although he couldn't move much the way Tilghman had him tied down.

Although the sound of a shot might still travel far enough to be noticed, Tilghman figured the man couldn't yell loud enough for his friends to hear him. He dismounted and stepped over beside the prisoner, who lifted his head and stared wild-eyed at him.

"Take it easy," Tilghman said. "If you cooperate with me, you won't be hurt any more than you already are, and you'll be treated fairly. I give you my word on that. I'll take this gag out so you can breathe a little easier."

He pulled the wad of wet cloth from the

man's mouth and tossed it aside. As he did so, a stream of profanity erupted from the prisoner. Tilghman let the rustler cuss, figuring he would run out of steam sooner or later.

He did. Panting in anger and outraged breathlessness, the man said, "I don't know who you are, mister . . . but you're gonna be sorry . . . you stuck your nose in where it ain't wanted. I'm gonna string you up by your heels . . . and roast your head over an open fire, the way the Apaches do."

"And you don't know who you're talking to," Tilghman said. "I'm a deputy United States marshal. It's probably not very smart to be threatening me like that."

"A deputy marshal . . . ! You're the one my brothers told me about."

Tilghman stiffened. There was only one reasonable explanation for the man's words.

By a stroke of pure luck, he had captured the very man he was looking for.

Cal Rainey, the ringleader of the rustlers.

Chapter 10

Tilghman smiled thinly in the darkness.

"Your brothers," he repeated. "I reckon you mean the mayor and the marshal of Burnt Creek."

Rainey must have realized that his anger had caused him to blurt out too much information. In a truculent voice, he said, "I don't know what the hell you're talking about."

"Sure you don't. You can deny it all you want, but I won't have any trouble finding folks in Burnt Creek who can identify you, and with my own ears I heard you admit to conspiring with Martin and Dave. All three of you will be going to prison for organizing this rustling ring . . . or to the gallows to pay for the men you murdered in your raids."

"You're loco, old man," Rainey growled. "I

don't know what you're talkin' about. I never killed anybody, and I never stole any cattle."

"What about that herd I saw you and your boys driving along the canyon?"

"That's my herd. You can check the brands on them. Boxed CR, every one."

"And if I shoot one of the varmints and peel the hide off it?" Tilghman said. "What'll I find then, Rainey? Evidence that the brands were tampered with? I haven't searched your saddlebags yet, but I wouldn't be surprised if I found a running iron in them."

Rainey's sullen silence told Tilghman he had probably guessed right about both of those things.

Evidence could wait, though. Right now the important thing was to get out of the hills and head back to Burnt Creek. Tilghman thought he could get there by dawn. If he could take Dave Rainey by surprise and get the drop on him, he could lock up Cal and Dave both in the local marshal's jail, then head over to the Drovers Hotel to round up Martin Rainey. With all three of the brothers behind bars, he could send word to Evett Nix asking for the reinforcements he would need to wrap up the job.

Tilghman picked up the gag he had discarded

earlier and said, "Open your mouth, Cal."

Rainey responded with a vile suggestion of several things Tilghman could do with the makeshift gag.

"You see, that's exactly why I don't want to have to listen to your filthy comments all the way back to Burnt Creek," Tilghman said. He took hold of Rainey's hair and jerked his head up. Rainey opened his mouth to yell, and Tilghman shoved the rag back in.

"It's your own fault," he pointed out. "I gave you a chance to act like a civilized human being."

Rainey just grunted furiously through the gag.

Tilghman mounted up and rode on, leading Rainey's horse. He steered by the stars and knew he was going in the right direction. Soon he would be out of the flat-topped hills and ridges and back on the open prairie, and then he could move even faster toward Burnt Creek.

A half-moon rose, spreading silvery illumination over the stark landscape. Because of that, Tilghman had a little warning when he spotted a moonbeam glinting off of something up ahead that wasn't a slab of gypsum. He leaned forward sharply as a rifle cracked. The bullet screamed through the air near his head, and he knew that if he hadn't ducked, he'd be dead right now.

He yanked his horse to the side and dug his heels into its flanks. The animal leaped ahead. Tilghman tightened his grip on the trailing horse's reins as he galloped toward some slabs of rock that had broken off from one of the hills in the past and slid down to form a cluster at its base. Those rocks wouldn't provide much cover, but they were better than nothing.

More shots blasted. Tilghman saw orange flame spurt from gun muzzles. None of the bullets came close to him, though. Hitting a swiftly moving target by moonlight was next thing to impossible. That first shot, when one of the bushwhackers had had time to draw a bead on him, had been their best chance.

The odds were still against him, though, and he knew it.

"Hold your fire, hold your fire!" a man shouted, his voice echoing back from the hillsides. "I think he's got Cal with him!"

Now they thought of that, Tilghman told himself with a faint, wry smile as he brought his mount to a skidding halt among the boulders. They were lucky they hadn't killed their boss already with a stray bullet.

For that matter, Tilghman realized, he didn't know if Cal Rainey was still alive. There hadn't been time to check.

He dismounted almost before his horse stopped moving and wrapped the other horse's reins around his saddlehorn, then pulled the Winchester from its scabbard. A slap on the rump made his mount move deeper into the rocks, taking the other horse with it. As they trotted off, Tilghman heard Rainey still making noises through the gag, so he knew the rustler chieftain was still alive.

Tilghman crouched behind one of the stone slabs. His keen eyes scanned the moon-dappled landscape that lay between his position and the next ridge. It was mostly open ground, but there were hummocks and rocks and gullies where bushwhackers could hide.

He had one small advantage over the rustlers. He knew he didn't have any allies out here, so any movement he saw would be that of an enemy.

Because of that, when he spotted a shape flitting through the shadows, he was able to press the rifle's trigger without hesitation. The weapon cracked, and he saw the moving shape tumble out of control. A howl of pain ripped through the night. From the sound of it, Tilghman knew he had hit the man, but probably hadn't wounded him mortally.

The shot drew plenty of return fire. Tilghman had to crouch even lower as slugs splattered against the rocks. Some of them bounced and whined off into the darkness. Some spent their force in a series of tinkling impacts and then clattered across the ground. It was a storm of lead, and Tilghman knew he would be lucky to come through it unscathed.

After a few nerve-wracking moments, the guns fell silent. The hush that followed as the echoes died away in the hills was eerie. In that tense quiet, Tilghman heard one of the men ask, "You think we got him?"

Tilghman thought about snapping a shot in the direction of the voice, but he eased off the pressure on the Winchester's trigger. If he fired, they would know for sure that he was still alive. This way he made them wonder about it. He might lure them into making a mistake that would turn the tide of battle.

For a long moment, nobody answered the rustler's question. Then another man called, "Garza! Scanlon! Work your way up along the flanks."

Scanlon, thought Tilghman. The young man Casey Spencer loved and wanted to marry, unless there was another Scanlon in the gang, which was possible, of course, but seemed unlikely to Tilghman. He had promised Casey he would do what he could for Scanlon, if he got the chance, but given the fact that the young man more than likely had just been doing his best to kill him, that possibility seemed pretty far-fetched at the moment.

Still, he didn't know for certain that Boone Scanlon had been one of the men shooting at him. The youngster could have held his fire.

Now Scanlon was one of the men ordered to catch him in a crossfire. Tilghman couldn't let that happen, no matter what he had told Casey. He watched for movement again, and after a moment he spotted a human shape wriggling across an open stretch of ground like a giant snake.

Tilghman put a bullet into the dirt less than a yard in front of the crawling man's head.

The rustler let out a startled yelp and leaped to his feet, clearly too startled to think straight. He had just made himself an even better target.

Tilghman didn't kill him, though. Instead he

sent a round whistling through the air near the man's head and made him leap for cover. Tilghman didn't know if he was shooting at Boone Scanlon or the rustler called Garza.

Either way, that moment of mercy might well come back to haunt him.

"Well, that tells us whether or not he's alive," the man who had spoken earlier said. He raised his voice and went on, "Mister, I don't know who you are, but can you hear me?"

They already knew where he was, so he wouldn't be giving anything away by answering. Staying low, he called, "I hear you! And I'm Deputy U.S. Marshal Bill Tilghman!"

That must have given them pause, because no one replied and there were no more shots for the moment. They were probably turning over the information in their brains, trying to figure out if they wanted to keep trying to kill a federal lawman or light a shuck out of there while they still could.

Finally, the spokesman called, "That's our boss you've got over there, Tilghman. Let him go and you can ride away from here."

A burst of muffled protest came from farther back in the rocks where the horses were. Tilghman figured Cal Rainey was disagreeing violently with that proposal.

"I'd say it's pretty unlikely you boys would do that," Tilghman replied. "I know what you've been up to and where your hiding place is. You're not going to let me live."

"You're wrong," the rustler said. "I'll be damned if I want a whole pack of federal lawdogs on my trail from now on, and that's what'll happen if we kill you. Might be time to cut our losses."

More likely, the man was thinking that he and his friends could drive the hidden herd north to Kansas as fast as they could, sell the cattle for whatever they would bring, and then scatter across the West. It wasn't a bad plan. Tilghman couldn't take on the whole gang and recover all that rustled stock by himself. By the time he could get any help, the outlaws would all be gone.

But he didn't trust any of the rustlers for a second, and anyway, it went against the grain for him to let a prisoner go, especially one like Cal Rainey who had been raising hell for quite a while and was responsible for the deaths of innocent people.

He had one card he might be able to play. He called, "Boone Scanlon!"

The silence that greeted the name had a shocked quality to it. A long moment ticked by, then a youthful voice shouted back, "How do you know who I am, Marshal?"

The rustler who had been doing all the talking snapped, "Shut up, Scanlon!"

"He already knows who I am, Jonah," Scanlon replied. He addressed Tilghman again. "What do you want, Marshal?"

"I talked to that gal of yours in town, Scanlon. Pretty little Casey Spencer. She wants to marry you, and I promised her I'd do what I can to see that that happens. But I can't help you as long as you're mixed up with this bunch of thieves and killers."

"By God, Scanlon, don't listen to him," the rustler called Jonah raged. "He's tryin' to turn you against us!"

And evidently there was a chance he might be able to do that, Tilghman thought. Otherwise Jonah wouldn't be so upset. Maybe Boone Scanlon was worth salvaging after all if his fellow outlaws didn't fully trust him.

"I'm telling you the truth, Boone!" Tilghman said. "My word carries a lot of weight in this territory. I can convince a judge to take it easy on you, as long as you haven't done anything too bad. But if you go along with the rest of this bunch, you'll wind up at the end of a hang rope just like them!"

"There's nothing I can do to help you, Marshal," Scanlon replied, but judging by the miserable sound of his voice, he wished that wasn't true. "You never should've come riding into the Devil's Hand!"

Tilghman was about to make another try at convincing the young rustler to switch sides, when he heard something behind him. Rocks slid and bounced, and that was enough to make him whirl around with the Winchester ready in his hands.

He caught a glimpse of a shape lunging toward him and knew that one of the gang had managed to get behind him and come down the hill. Tilghman fired, and at the same time Colt flame bloomed in the darkness, practically right in his face, blinding him. The shot was deafening. Combined, those two things plunged him into a world where he couldn't see or hear and could only strike out wildly with the faint hope of hitting anything.

An instant later, something smashed into the side of his head. The impact drove him back against the boulder behind him. His strength deserted him. He felt his legs folding up underneath him, but there was nothing he could do to stop himself from sliding into black oblivion.

Chapter 11

Terrible heat pounded into Tilghman's face like a fiery fist, and the glare of leaping flames assaulted his eyes when he forced them open. For a second he thought he was dead and in Hell, which didn't seem right. He had tried to lead a moral, God-fearing life.

But he had killed a number of men in the course of his work, and even though he considered those deaths justified under man's law, the Good Lord might not feel the same way. After all, the Bible said, "Thou shalt not kill," and didn't set out any exceptions to that rule.

The Bible also specified an eye for an eye and a tooth for a tooth and made it plain that those who lived by the sword would die by the sword, which Tilghman had always figured applied by extension to six-guns, too.

None of that theological pondering mattered, he realized, because he wasn't dead after all. He had flinched a little from the flames, and that brought a bray of laughter from somebody nearby.

"It's about time you woke up, Tilghman," a familiar voice said. "I told you I was gonna burn you like the Apaches do, but I want you to know what's goin' on when your brain starts to fry."

That would be Cal Rainey, thought Tilghman. He squinted through narrowed eyes that were starting to adjust to the garish firelight. Several tall, man-shaped figures loomed around him. He realized that he was lying on the ground, looking up at them.

As his vision cleared even more, he began to make out his captors' faces. The one standing in front of him, leering down at him with such a cruel, satisfied expression, had to be Cal Rainey. With the red, flickering light from the fire washing over his rawboned face, Rainey looked positively Satanic.

Three more men stood nearby. One of them was short and chunky, with a rust-colored beard. Another was a half-breed wearing a hat with a low, round crown and a turquoise-studded band. A blood-stained bandanna tied around his thigh meant he was probably the man Tilghman had winged earlier.

The final man was the youngest of the bunch, with a shock of black hair and a worried face under a pushed-back Stetson. Tilghman pegged him as being Boone Scanlon. He was the only one who looked like a cowboy recently gone bad. The others were veteran desperadoes.

The night was still black except where the fire burned. Tilghman found the half-moon in the sky. He could tell by its location that he had been unconscious for quite a while.

His head pounded from the blow that had knocked him out. He didn't know if a bullet had grazed his skull or if he'd been walloped by a gun or some other weapon. In the end, it didn't really matter, he supposed.

His arms were twisted awkwardly and uncomfortably behind him. When he tried to move them he found that his wrists were tied securely. So were his ankles. They had trussed him up good and proper. This was about the most hopeless position in which he had ever found himself.

He wished he'd had a chance to tell Flora goodbye. But they had always known that whenever he rode away from the ranch on law business, there was a chance he wouldn't be coming back.

That despairing thought went through his brain, but the next second he angrily shoved it away. Thinking about regrets meant that he was giving up, and he wasn't going to do that as long as there was breath left in his body.

Cal Rainey said, "Garza, you head on back to the others and let them know what's going on. We'll catch up with the herd once we're finished with the marshal here."

The 'breed nodded solemnly, his bronzed face expressionless. He turned and limped over to some horses, swung up into the saddle of one of them, and rode away.

Rainey went to the horses, too, and came back with a coiled lariat. It was the same one Tilghman had used to tie him onto his horse. Rainey must be taking some pleasure from that irony, the lawman thought.

Whistling a tuneless air between his teeth, Rainey hunkered beside Tilghman's bound feet and fastened one end of the lariat around his ankles. The outlaw with the rust-colored beard, who had to be Jonah, stood watching stolidly, as did Scanlon.

When Rainey had the rope tied to his

satisfaction, he stood and tossed the other end over a big slab of rock. They had built the fire at the base of that rock.

"All right, you two," Rainey said. "Go around on the other side and haul him up. I'll lift him on this side so you won't drag him through the fire. We don't want this gettin' over with too soon."

When the Apaches suspended their torture victims head-down over a fire, they usually built some sort of platform from which to dangle them, or else used a tree limb. There weren't enough trees out here to do either of those things, so Rainey had come up with another method for taking his cruel revenge on Tilghman.

It ought to work, too. The rock was about twelve feet tall. The two men on the other end of the rope would be able to lift him high enough that he wouldn't burn right away. Instead he would roast slowly over the flames until his brain burst. And he would be awake and aware for most of it.

It would be an awful way to die.

"Come on, kid," Jonah said.

Tilghman said, "You don't have to do this, Boone. Think about how Casey would feel if she knew. You reckon she'd still want to marry you?"

The toe of Rainey's boot jabbed into Tilghman's side in a brutal kick.

"Shut up, lawman," Rainey said. "Ol' Boone here knows who his friends really are. He wouldn't ever double-cross us. Ain't that right, Boone?"

Scanlon swallowed hard and licked his lips. He said, "I'm sorry, Marshal. Like I told you before, you shouldn't have come out here huntin' us."

"Get goin'," Rainey snapped. "I'm ready to see this badge-toter get what's comin' to him."

Tilghman said, "Your brother's a lawman, too, Rainey, don't forget that."

Another burst of harsh laughter came from Rainey.

"Just because an hombre pins on a badge don't mean anything, and politicians are bigger crooks than all the rustlers and road agents put together. My brothers are livin' proof of that!"

"They were in on it with you from the first, weren't they?"

"Hell, it was all Mart's idea. We all rode together when we were pullin' jobs in Missouri and Arkansas. Then he decided he wanted to get respectable and talked Dave into comin' out here with him. He built that damned hotel and saloon and even got hisself elected mayor. Got Dave the marshal's job. But when it didn't work out, it didn't take him long at all to go back to the old ways! He sent for me, told me to get a gang together and we'd clean up. So far we have been, too." A shrewd look came into Rainey's eyes. "And you're just tryin' to get me to talk to keep from gettin' your brain cooked for that much longer. But it's not gonna work." He turned to Scanlon and Jonah. "I told you two to get on the other end of that rope!"

"We're goin'," Jonah said. He walked around the big rock.

Boone Scanlon followed more reluctantly, casting a glance back at Tilghman as he did so. Tilghman didn't say anything, but his solemn gaze was a mute reminder of Casey Spencer.

At least, he hoped so. That slender thread was the only thing he had to cling to.

The rope at Tilghman's feet grew taut. He started sliding toward the fire. Rainey moved behind him, bent down, got hold of him under the arms and lifted him. His feet kept rising until he was almost upside down. With most of his weight on the rope, Rainey was able to maneuver him around the fire, then let go of him and give him a shove that sent him crashing against the rock face.

The flames were right below him. Tilghman's lips drew back from his teeth in a grimace as the terrible heat surrounded him. He expected his hair to catch on fire at any second.

"Haul him up higher!" Rainey yelled. "I'll tell you when to stop!"

Tilghman's head bumped painfully against the rock as he rose a couple of feet. The heat was only marginally better. He knew he wouldn't last long like this. Already it felt like his eyeballs were about to explode.

"A little more! There, that's good! Hold him right there!"

Tilghman came to a stop with his head about five feet above the fire. This was the worst thing he had ever experienced. But he still wasn't going to give up.

He had to draw in a deep breath in order to shout, and the super-heated air seemed to sear his lungs. He yelled, "Boone! You can still stop this!"

"Shut up, lawdog!" Rainey yelled. He cackled as he drew his gun and pulled back the hammer. The revolver roared twice. A bullet slammed into the rock face on either side of Tilghman, just a couple of feet away. Little slivers of rock stung his face. "By the time you're good an' cooked, you'll be beggin' me to put you out of your misery! But I won't do it, no, sir!"

Two more shots blasted into the rock around Tilghman as Rainey continued to torment the lawman. Then another report sounded, but it didn't come from Rainey's gun. Tilghman's heart leaped in his chest as he realized it came from the other side of the boulder.

A split-second later, he plummeted toward the flames beneath him as the rope, loose now, slithered over the top of the rock.

Chapter 12

Tilghman twisted desperately in mid-air as he fell so that he wouldn't land directly on his head and probably break his neck. He crashed into the fire on his left shoulder first and rolled. Flames licked at his exposed skin and made him want to scream.

He gritted his teeth and swung his legs to kick out at Cal Rainey as the boss rustler charged up to the very edge of the fire. The blow swept Rainey's legs out from under him and dumped him in the flames as well. Rainey yelled as he toppled into the fire.

Tilghman got his feet against the ground and shoved as hard as he could in an attempt to get away from the blaze. His clothes were smoldering now. He rolled over and over on the dirt, smothering the tiny flames that began to leap up.

He had scattered the burning branches when he landed among them. One lay only a couple of feet away. Tilghman put his back to it and thrust his hands as far behind him as he could, holding the ropes in the flames that still danced along the wood.

Again he wanted to scream from the pain as the fire blistered his skin, but he felt the strands around his wrists weakening. The muscles in his arms and shoulders bunched under his coat as he heaved against the burning rope as hard as he could.

It parted, and suddenly his arms were free. He looked around and saw Rainey scrambling clear of the fire, yelling and cussing as he did so.

Between them lay the revolver that Rainey had dropped when Tilghman kicked his feet out from under him.

Desperation, fueled as well by the anger Tilghman felt over the hell Rainey had put him through, gave the lawman a slight edge as he lunged toward the gun. He reached it first and scooped it up in both hands. His fingers were partially numb from his wrists being tied and didn't want to work right. They felt swollen and clumsy.

But he managed to tip the barrel up and pull the hammer back as Rainey charged toward him. Tilghman got a finger on the trigger and squeezed.

The gun bucked in his hands as it blasted a bullet through Rainey's shoulder. Blood flew in the air as the slug's impact drove Rainey backward.

Over the roaring of his pulse in his head, Tilghman heard rapid footsteps rushing toward him. He rolled and twisted and brought the gun up again. He didn't know if Rainey was in the habit of carrying the hammer on an empty chamber. If he was, that meant the gun was empty.

Tilghman didn't have to find out. A few yards away, Boone Scanlon came to a sliding stop and cried, "Don't shoot, Marshal!" He had a gun in his hand, but he dropped it and thrust both arms skyward. "Don't shoot, I came to help you!"

Tilghman believed him. He dropped Rainey's gun and pushed himself into a sitting position.

"Pick up your gun and cover Rainey," he told Scanlon as he began fumbling with the bonds around his ankles. "I don't know how bad he's hit."

Scanlon hesitated for a second, then did as Tilghman told him. He retrieved his gun, pointed it at the fallen Rainey, and dug in his pocket with his left hand. When he brought out a clasp knife, he tossed it on the ground next to Tilghman.

"Try that, Marshal," he said. "You might have better luck."

Tilghman picked up the knife. It took a minute for him to get the blade open. When he did, he started sawing on the ropes that fastened his ankles together.

"What about Jonah?" he asked Scanlon.

The young man looked a little sick as he choked out, "He's dead. First man I ever killed. And the last one, I hope."

"I hope so, too, kid," Tilghman said. The rope fell away from his legs as he finished cutting through the twisted strands.

"I just couldn't let Cal go through with it," Scanlon went on. "I told Jonah we had to help you. I started to let go of the rope, but he hung on to it with one hand while he made a grab for his gun with the other. I got mine out first and shot him." Scanlon shook his head. "When we both let go of the rope, that dumped you right in the fire, didn't it?"

"The burns I got will heal," Tilghman told him. "The way things were going, I wouldn't have lasted much longer. You saved my life, Boone, and shooting Jonah was self-defense. If you were telling me the truth about never killing anybody else, I can help you with the court, just like I said."

"It's true, all right, but I did rustle a heap of cattle," Scanlon said gloomily.

"And saved a federal marshal's life. I'd like to think that's worth something."

Tilghman had been letting the blood flow back into his feet as he talked, restoring the feeling in those mostly numb extremities. Now he climbed a little unsteadily to his feet and checked Rainey's gun.

Empty, just like he'd suspected. But it was a .45 like the one Tilghman carried, so fresh cartridges from the loops on the lawman's shell belt fit the chambers just fine.

When he had the gun reloaded, he stepped over to Rainey, who lay on the ground clutching his bullet-shattered shoulder and whimpering. There was a lot of blood on Rainey's shirt, soaking the sleeve down to the elbow.

"It's a long ride back to Guthrie," Tilghman said as he tore strips off the bottom of Rainey's shirt and started using them to bind up the wounded shoulder as best he could. "If I try to take Rainey there, he probably won't make it. There's a doctor in Burnt Creek, though, isn't there?"

"Yeah," Scanlon said, "but Mayor Rainey and the marshal are there, too."

"Well, I'll just have to deal with them when the time comes," Tilghman said with a thin smile. "You want to help me get Cal on his horse?"

"After what I did for you, you expect me to go back with you and face the law?"

Tilghman said, "I expect you to do that for your own sake, not mine, Boone. If you run now, you'll spend the rest of your life on the run. There won't be any way you can ever marry Casey and have a family with her. But if you go back and face whatever you've got coming to you, face it like a man, the two of you can start over. I'm not saying it'll be easy. It won't. But you can do it and still build a life worth having."

A small, bitter laugh escaped from Scanlon's lips. He said, "Are you a star packer or a sky pilot, Marshal Tilghman?"

He shook his head, indicating that Tilghman didn't have to answer, and holstered his gun. "You take his feet. I'll get his shoulders."

"Careful of the busted one."

"After what he did, I'd think that you'd want to cause him as much pain as possible."

"That's not the way I do things," Tilghman said. "He's my prisoner now, so I'll take care of him the best I can."

"Am I your prisoner?" Scanlon asked as he bent to get a grip under the wounded rustler's shoulders.

Tilghman took hold of Rainey's ankles and said, "We'll talk about that later."

They lifted Rainey into the saddle, setting him upright this time. Tilghman tied Rainey's wrists to the saddle horn. Rainey was only half-conscious and swayed on the horse's back.

"We'll ride close beside him on either side and keep him from falling off," Tilghman told Scanlon. He had already seen that his horse was with the other mounts, having been recovered from the rocks where he had taken cover earlier.

Minutes later, after Tilghman kicked out the last few burning branches from the fire that had almost been his death pyre, they rode away from the place. Tilghman's hat was gone, but he wasn't going to waste time looking for it.

"Was it Garza who got behind me and jumped me back there in the rocks?" he asked Scanlon.

"Yeah. You'd winged him, but he said he could do it anyway. Jonah told him to give it a try."

"Were you the fella who tried to crawl across that open stretch in front of me?"

Scanlon grunted and said, "Yeah. I reckon you scared me out of a year's growth when those shots came so close to me, Marshal. It's a good thing the light wasn't any better or you would have ventilated me for sure."

"The light was plenty good," Tilghman drawled. "I was trying to miss you, son. I don't kill unless I have to, and tonight that habit paid off. If I'd drilled you, you wouldn't have been around to help me, and I reckon I'd be roast meat by now."

"Funny how things work out, ain't it?"

"You could say that." Tilghman paused, then asked, "How did the three of you come to be after us? I thought I'd grabbed Rainey without anybody knowing about it."

"He'd told Jonah to keep the cattle moving on

to the next canyon where we were gonna graze them, but Jonah turned back to ask him something and got there in time to see you riding off with the boss slung over his saddle. Garza and I were the first ones Jonah found when he went to look for some help. Garza knows these parts better than anybody. He suggested we get around in front of you and set up an ambush. It nearly worked. I don't know what warned you he was about to shoot, Marshal."

"Instinct," Tilghman said. "I saw moonlight reflect off something and figured it was a rifle barrel. That's what made me duck."

"Yeah, but that reflection could've been anything."

"I suppose it could have. And if it had turned out to be harmless, I might've felt a little foolish about reacting the way I did. But I'd have still been alive, wouldn't I?"

Scanlon laughed softly and said, "You're right about that. I guess when you've been a lawman for a long time, you learn that it's better to be careful."

"That's what keeps us alive. That . . . and a big helping of good luck."

The half-breed Garza might know the Devil's

Hand better than anyone else, according to Scanlon, but the young cowboy-turned-outlaw was pretty familiar with the area, too. He led Tilghman out of the stretch of rugged hills and pointed them toward the settlement. Tilghman wasn't sure anymore that they could reach Burnt Creek by morning, but he was still going to try.

After they had ridden for a while, Scanlon asked, "How are you acquainted with Casey, Marshal?"

"She waited on me in the hotel dining room. And then she snuck into my room last night and asked me to help you. She's been mighty worried about you, son."

"Yeah, that sounds like her," Scanlon said. "I tried to tell her for a while that I was no good, that she could do a whole heap better than me, but she wouldn't listen. She's got a mind of her own. How'd she know I've been riding with Cal and his bunch?"

"She figured it out," Tilghman said. "I don't reckon it was that hard."

"Yeah, she's smart, too. She's a lot better than an owlhoot like me deserves."

"Then don't be an owlhoot anymore. Earn the way she feels about you."

"That's a lot easier said than done."

"Most things worth doing aren't very easy."

Rainey hadn't made any sounds for a while except an occasional low moan. Now he said disgustedly, "Will you two shut up? I'm bleedin' to death here, and you're yammerin' about some girl!"

"Don't expect any sympathy from me, Rainey," Tilghman snapped. "Some men would've just put a bullet in your head and made things a lot simpler."

"You can't do that, though, can you? High an' mighty lawman. My brothers'll do for you. You don't know what you're ridin' into, Tilghman."

"We'll find out soon enough," Tilghman said. "As soon as we get back to Burnt Creek."

Chapter 13

The eastern sky was gray with the approach of dawn as Tilghman, Scanlon, and Cal Rainey neared the settlement. Tilghman had hoped to reach Burnt Creek earlier than this, increasing the chances of surprising Dave Rainey and taking him prisoner, but under the circumstances he considered himself lucky to be alive, so he couldn't complain too much.

He reined to a halt while they were still several hundred yards away and brought Rainey's horse to a stop as well. Scanlon followed suit.

"We don't want Rainey doing any yelling when we ride in," Tilghman said. "Boone, use your bandanna to gag him."

Rainey let out a string of curses at the idea of being gagged again. Scanlon cut off the flow of profanity by shoving his bandanna in the boss rustler's mouth and tying it behind Rainey's head.

"Now he can't alert his brothers," Tilghman said. "Come on. We need to make it to the back of the jail. Maybe I can get the drop on Dave."

"And lock him up in one of his own cells, along with Cal?" Scanlon nodded. "That sounds like a good idea."

Something occurred to Tilghman. He asked, "What do you know about the deputy?"

"Coley Barnett? We used to punch cattle together, before he went into the law business and I went . . . Well, we both know where I went."

"But is he part of the gang? Does he know what the Rainey brothers have really been up to?"

"I'd bet a hat that he doesn't," Scanlon said. "Coley's honest as the day is long. Dave Rainey's been using him to take care of the marshal's duties while Dave sits back and collects his share of the loot from the rustling and the robberies."

"Would he believe you if you told him what's been going on?"

Scanlon rubbed his chin and frowned in thought.

"Maybe," he said. "We always got along well. And I reckon he'd sure take the word of a deputy U.S. marshal."

"Then if we run into any trouble, we might be able to get some help from him."

"Yeah, I think there's a good chance of that," Scanlon agreed.

Tilghman nodded and said, "We'd better get busy, then, before it gets any lighter. It's already late enough that quite a few folks will be up and around."

"Dave Rainey shouldn't be one of them. From what I've heard Cal say about him, Dave's not one to get up early."

That was encouraging. Tilghman heeled his horse into motion again. They rode through the gray dawn toward the town, where lights were beginning to appear in some of the windows.

Their route took them past the livery stable. The big double doors were closed, but one of them swung open as the three riders passed. Raoul Gonzalez stepped out, yawning sleepily and stretching. He stopped in mid-yawn and his eyes widened as much as his mouth was when he saw Tilghman, Scanlon, and Rainey.

"¡Caramba!" he exclaimed softly. "Señor Marshal Tilghman, is that – "

"It is," Tilghman said. An idea occurred to him. "Señor Gonzalez, I need to use your barn for a few minutes."

He motioned for Scanlon and Rainey to ride into the cavernous building.

Gonzalez hurriedly opened the other door to give them plenty of room. He was clearly nervous as he said, "Señor Marshal, what are you doing?"

"I'm going to leave these two here while I go to the jail," Tilghman said. "I'll stand a better chance of not attracting attention if I'm by myself."

"You trust me that much, Marshal?" Scanlon asked.

"I don't have much choice in the matter. Anyway, you've done enough to tell me that you'd rather be on the side of the law, Boone. Now you've got that chance."

Scanlon nodded and promised solemnly, "I won't let you down."

Gonzalez motioned toward the prisoner and said, "This is Cal Rainey, señor."

"I know that. He's the boss of that rustling ring. One of the bosses, anyway. I'm on my way to round up the other two now."

"I don't have to ask who you mean," Gonzalez said. "You should be very careful. Mayor Rainey, he has quite a few men who work for him. Men who are not good, if you know what I mean."

"I'll keep my eyes open," Tilghman said. "I'll be back as soon as I've got the other two under lock and key. Raoul, do you think you can go and fetch the doctor here without telling him what's going on? I don't want a commotion raised just yet."

"Sí, I will try," Gonzalez promised with a bob of his head. "Your hands and face are burned, Señor Marshal. You need the doctor yourself."

"All in good time, Señor Gonzalez, all in good time."

Tilghman left his horse in the barn with the others and went back out into the street. It was a couple of blocks to the town marshal's office, not far at all. He knew it would be a nerve-wracking walk, though.

Tilghman turned the corner and started along one of the blocks facing the square. Lights were burning in the hotel. In the kitchen and dining room, the people who worked there were probably getting ready for breakfast, including

Casey Spencer.

Tilghman wished he could see her for a moment and let her know that Scanlon was all right. He didn't have time for that, though. He needed to get to the jail. He could see it just ahead of him . . .

The sound of hoofbeats made him pause and look around. The sun still wasn't up, but there was already enough light in the sky for him to gaze out onto the prairie and see a large group of horsemen galloping toward the settlement. A cloud of dust boiled up from the hooves of their racing mounts.

Tilghman knew instantly who those riders had to be. Garza must have returned to the place where Cal Rainey intended to wreak his terrible vengeance on the lawman. Finding Tilghman, Rainey, and Scanlon gone and Jonah dead, Garza would have known that something unexpected had happened. He must have gathered up the rest of the gang and followed the trail here to town.

As those thoughts flashed through Tilghman's mind, he turned away from the jail, whirled around, and broke into a run back toward the livery stable. He didn't have time to deal with Dave Rainey right now. Garza and the other rustlers would be here in a matter of minutes.

Nor could he and Scanlon hole up in the barn and hope to fight off the gang. The place wasn't made to defend against a large, well-armed force.

Tilghman had an idea for a refuge that might be better. He had to hurry, though.

The stable doors were closed almost all the way. Gonzalez hadn't left yet to fetch the doctor and must have been keeping a watch through the narrow crack between the doors because one side suddenly started to swing open as Tilghman approached. As he rushed into the barn he was glad to see that Scanlon and Rainey were still mounted.

"Come on!" Tilghman called to them as he practically leaped into his saddle. "We're headed for the hotel!"

"The hotel!" Scanlon repeated as Tilghman led the charge out of the barn. "What – "

"The rest of the gang will be here any minute!" Tilghman flung over his shoulder. "We're going to fort up on the top floor of the hotel."

"But Casey – "

"She'll be safe as long as she clears out and

lays low. We'll grab Martin when we go in, so we'll have both him and Cal to use as hostages."

There was no time to explain any more than that. The horses pounded around the corner. Tilghman didn't slow down as he approached the hotel. He headed for the steps and rode right up onto the verandah with Scanlon behind him, leading Cal Rainey's horse. Rainey yelled through his gag, but the sounds were muffled and incoherent and lost in the clatter of horseshoes on the planks of the verandah.

Tilghman's mount tried to shy away from the doors, but Tilghman jerked his right foot from the stirrup, kicked the doors open, and sent the animal crashing on through into the lobby, ducking his head as he did so to clear the top of the opening. He heard a shout of alarm from the desk clerk.

Tilghman dismounted quickly, pulled his saddlebags loose and slung them over his shoulder, and turned to the horse carrying Cal Rainey. Scanlon was already leaning over in the saddle, using his knife to cut the bonds holding Rainey's wrists to the saddle horn. Tilghman grabbed Rainey and hauled him off the horse.

"Boone!"

The woman's surprised shout made

Tilghman glance around. He saw Casey rush out of the dining room toward them. Scanlon slipped down from his horse's back and grabbed her as she threw herself into his arms.

"Casey, honey," Scanlon said as he hugged her tightly to him. "It's all right, Casey, but you've gotta get out of here."

She drew back a little and shook her head vehemently as she looked up at him.

"I'm not going anywhere except with you," she told him. "It's about time you understood that."

Tilghman drew his gun and used his other hand to grab Rainey's uninjured arm. He forced the rustler toward the stairs and said over his shoulder, "You two will have to work this out later. Come on, Boone."

Scanlon kissed Casey and then pushed her away.

"Please," he begged her, "get out of here and go somewhere safe."

Then he turned and backed toward the stairs, covering the open doors with his gun as he did so.

Rainey didn't cooperate. He struggled and made it as difficult as possible for Tilghman to force him up the stairs. Tilghman felt like bending the gun barrel over his head, but he knew that knocking Rainey unconscious wouldn't help matters. Then he'd have to deal with the outlaw's dead weight.

Wounded and weakened like he was, though, Rainey couldn't put up too much of a fight as Tilghman wrestled him up the stairs. They reached the second floor landing. Tilghman turned and started up toward the third floor.

The scuff of shoe leather against the floor warned him. He looked up as Martin Rainey appeared at the top of the stairs. Martin had a pistol in his hand, and he sized up the situation instantly. Seeing his brother Cal as Tilghman's prisoner told him that there was no point in pretending to be an honest businessman any longer. He snapped up the pistol and jerked the trigger.

At the same time, Tilghman shoved Cal Rainey down to get him out of the line of fire. The bullet from Martin's gun whipped past Tilghman's ear as he crouched. He squeezed off a round of his own, aiming carefully, and Martin cried out and staggered as the lawman's bullet ripped through his right thigh. He almost fell, but he caught his balance and tried to raise his gun again.

He stopped when he saw Tilghman gazing intently at him over the barrel of the Colt .45 in the marshal's hand.

"I don't want to kill you, Rainey," Tilghman said, "but the next one goes in your head if you don't drop that gun."

Martin's pistol thudded to the floor.

Tilghman hoisted Cal Rainey to his feet again and resumed the climb. Boone Scanlon was close behind them, still covering their ascent.

"Back away from the landing," Tilghman ordered. Martin did so, holding his wounded leg with both hands now and limping heavily. His face was pale with shock and pain.

"What . . . what . . . " he managed to say.

"You know good and well what's going on here," Tilghman snapped. "You and your brother are my prisoners. You're going to answer for all the rustling you've done, as well as the men you've killed. I reckon there's a good chance you'll both swing, but you never know. You might just spend the rest of your lives behind bars."

"You . . . you can't do this. You're just one man – "

"There are two of us," Scanlon said. "I'm backing the marshal's play."

"And so am I," a new voice said.

Tilghman swung around to see Raoul Gonzalez coming along the third floor balcony toward them with a shotgun in his hands. The stableman went on, "There is a rear staircase, Señor Marshal, but don't worry, I'll make sure no one comes up that way. When I heard you say you were coming up here, I knew you would need help."

Since Gonzalez was a civilian, Tilghman's first impulse was to send him away, out of the line of fire. But Gonzalez was right. He and Scanlon would need help to hold off the rest of the gang. He nodded to Gonzalez and said, "Muchas gracias, señor. I just hope you don't get yourself killed."

"A wish I devoutly share for us all!"

Tilghman shoved Martin Rainey into a chair. The mayor was wearing a dressing gown with a belt tied around its middle. Tilghman took the belt off and used it to tie him into the chair.

"We don't need you running around loose, Mayor," he said.

"I'm wounded," Martin wailed. "I'm going to bleed to death!"

"Maybe not. If you're lucky."

Tilghman tied Cal Rainey into another chair.

He had just finished doing that when he heard the swift rataplan of hoofbeats in the street outside.

"They're here. Let's find some windows and give 'em a warm welcome!"

Chapter 14

Since the third floor was devoted entirely to Martin Rainey's personal quarters, the rooms were much larger than the other rooms in the hotel. Along the front of the building were a sitting room and a dining room, with Rainey's bedroom in the back. Tilghman and Scanlon ran into the sitting room while Gonzalez retreated along the corridor to cover the rear stairwell.

Tilghman would have liked to have some rifles at their disposal, but the reality was that he and Scanlon were armed only with a six-gun each. The good thing was that they had plenty of ammunition, at least for the moment. Tilghman had a couple of boxes of .45s in his saddlebags.

Dust swirled in the street outside as

Tilghman and Scanlon reached the sitting room windows. Tilghman spotted Garza, who seemed to have taken over temporary command of the gang. They had reined in, and the half-breed was looking around, as if trying to decide what to do next.

Someone was bound to tell them about the three men riding into the hotel lobby on horseback, so there was no hope they could hide up here and not be discovered. Better not to waste the element of surprise, Tilghman decided.

He shoved the window up, thrust the Colt through the opening, and fired.

The bullet struck Garza and rocked him in the saddle. At the window next to Tilghman, Scanlon opened fire as well. His shot knocked one of the rustlers to the ground. Each of them managed to squeeze off another shot before return fire drove them back from the windows. Tilghman knelt, edged forward, and sent two more bullets screaming into the mass of outlaws in the street.

"How many do you reckon are out there?" he called over to Scanlon.

"At least twenty," the young man replied.

"Ten to one odds, then." Tilghman grinned.

"Could be worse!"

Not many of Burnt Creek's citizens had been on the street this early, and once the shooting started, those who were cleared out in a hurry. Tilghman was glad to see them scurrying for cover. He didn't want any innocents injured if it could be avoided.

The outlaws began to scatter as well. Some of them tried to reach the hotel's verandah so they could get inside the building, but accurate fire from Tilghman and Scanlon drove them back. They wound up taking cover behind water troughs and parked wagons and inside buildings across the street facing the hotel.

Once they were behind shelter, they started sniping at the third floor windows with rifles and pistols. Bullets shattered the windows and sent shards of glass spraying across the room, causing Tilghman and Scanlon to duck again. As soon as all the windows were busted out, though, at least they didn't have to worry about that anymore.

"They're going to try to get around behind us," Scanlon warned during a lull in the firing. Strands of gray powdersmoke floated in the room.

"Even if they do, they can't get to us without

coming up those back stairs," Tilghman said. "As long as Raoul is waiting there with that scattergun of his, I don't think they're going to have much luck."

He took a box of cartridges from his saddlebags and slid them across the floor to Scanlon. Both men took advantage of the opportunity to fill the cylinders of their guns.

A footstep behind them made Tilghman spin around and lift his Colt. He didn't think either Cal or Martin Rainey could have gotten loose, but anything was possible.

What he saw took him even more by surprise. Casey Spencer stood there with a Winchester in each hand.

"I found these downstairs and thought you could use them," she said.

Scanlon leaped to his feet.

"Blast it, Casey!" he exclaimed. "I thought I told you to get – "

At that moment the outlaws across the street opened fire again, pouring lead at the hotel's top floor. Scanlon dived at Casey and tackled her, pulling her to the floor as bullets began to zip through the broken windows. She was far enough back so that the shots probably would have missed her anyway, because of the angle at which they were fired, but Scanlon clearly didn't want to risk that.

Casey yelped in fear as she hit the floor. She said, "I'm sorry, Boone. I didn't mean to cause trouble. But I'm going to help you, whether you want my help or not!"

"And we're obliged to you," Tilghman told her. "Those rifles will come in handy, all right. Slide one of 'em over here, Boone."

Scanlon did so. The Winchesters held fifteen .45 caliber rounds apiece, more than twice as much as the Colts. That would help considerably. And having Casey here meant they had an extra pair of hands that could be busy reloading while Tilghman and Scanlon were making things hot for the enemy. Tilghman would have preferred that Casey had gotten out of the hotel and hunkered down somewhere safe, but since she hadn't, they might as well take advantage of her offer to help.

He filled the rifle that Scanlon pushed over to him, then came up on his knees and thrust the barrel over the windowsill. The Winchester blasted a string of half a dozen shots as fast as Tilghman could work the weapon's lever and pull the trigger. He sprayed lead across the front of the building across the street and around a wagon where he knew at least one of the rustlers had taken cover. The barrage had an effect, as a man flopped out from behind the wagon and writhed in the dirt from the pain of being wounded in the side. He tried to crawl back into cover but didn't make it in time. Tilghman drilled him through the head.

Heavy return fire forced the lawman to drop below the window again. He looked over at Scanlon as the young man returned to the other window.

"Do you know how many men Dave Rainey can muster here in town who work for him and his brothers?"

Scanlon shook his head and said, "I don't have any idea. Another dozen, maybe?"

Tilghman thought of something else that made a grim look settle over his face.

"That's not all we have to worry about," he said. "Most of the folks in town don't know what all the shooting is about. Dave can tell them anything he wants to. He can convince them that a couple of outlaws are holed up in the hotel and get volunteers to join the fight."

"Innocent folks, you mean?"

"That's right. He may try to turn all of Burnt

Creek against us."

"I'm not gonna shoot innocent people," Scanlon declared. "Although . . . how will we know?" A look of despair came over his rugged young features. "We can't win, Marshal. There's just no way. Not with all of the gang and the whole town against us."

He was probably right, thought Tilghman. If he'd had a little more time and had been able to get all three of the Rainey brothers behind bars, he would have been able to explain the truth to the rest of the citizens and enlist their help when the gang came storming into town. But that hadn't worked out, and now all the odds were stacked against them.

The only card he had left to play was that he had Cal and Martin Rainey as his prisoners. That might give him a little bargaining power. Also, people in town knew who he was. Would they take the word of a deputy U.S. marshal over that of their local lawman? Tilghman didn't know, but it was worth a try. He just had to get the truth out there somehow.

The boom of a shotgun filled the air and made Casey jump. Tilghman crawled across the floor to the sitting room door, trying to avoid the broken glass as he did so. Leading with the

Winchester, he stuck his head and shoulders into the hall. It was empty except for Cal and Martin Rainey, tied into the chairs where they sat.

"Señor Gonzalez!" Tilghman called. "You all right down there?"

"Sí, señor," came the stableman's answer. "A couple of those badmen, they tried to come up the stairs."

"What happened?"

"They were not expecting me to be waiting for them. They will not go back down under their own power. They will have to be carried down."

"Good job." Tilghman got to his feet and edged along the wall toward the prisoners. He came to Cal Rainey first, who cursed him bitterly as Tilghman loosened the ropes and jerked him to his feet. Tilghman said, "Come on. I've got work for you to do."

"If you think I'll help you, you damn lawdog – "

Tilghman put the Winchester's muzzle under Cal's chin.

"I haven't forgotten what you tried to do to me up there in the Devil's Hand," he grated. "These burns I've got sting like blazes, and I'll carry the scars from them for the rest of my life. What I need you for is to keep your friends from shooting at me, and you can do that dead as well as alive. You'd be wise to remember that."

Cal didn't say anything else as Tilghman shoved him along the hall to the door of the sitting room. The gunfire had tapered off again. This was the time to make his move.

Tilghman rushed Cal Rainey across the room to the window. It went against the grain for him to use a man as a human shield, even a rustler and killer like Rainey. There was a chance the outlaws would open fire as soon as Cal appeared in the opening, without waiting to see who he was. Tilghman had to run that risk. Circumstances had already forced him into doing the sort of things he normally went out of his way to avoid, such as riding those horses right into the hotel lobby like some sort of Wild West showman.

"Hold your fire! Hold your fire!" somebody bellowed across the street as Tilghman held Cal Rainey in front of him. "That's the boss!"

"Dave Rainey!" Tilghman shouted over Cal's shoulder. "Dave, I know you're out there somewhere! You'd better answer me!" He paused, then added, "This is Deputy United States Marshal William Tilghman!"

The guns were all silent now. Tilghman knew

his powerful voice would carry along the street. He hoped that a number of Burnt Creek citizens would hear it and start to realize that the situation wasn't exactly what their local marshal must have told them it was.

A moment of silence ticked past, then Dave Rainey replied from the building across the street, where he had joined forces with Garza and the other rustlers.

"What do you want, Tilghman, if that's who you really are?"

A bleak smile tugged briefly at Tilghman's mouth under his mustache. That was neatly played on Dave's part, he thought. Dave was trying to cast doubt on Tilghman's identity so maybe he could keep the townspeople on his side.

"You can see for yourself that your brother is my prisoner," Tilghman called. "So is your other brother Martin. They're in federal custody, and you'd do well to surrender before anyone else gets hurt."

"You're a crook and a murderer!" Dave responded. "Why else would you kidnap my brothers? They hadn't done anything wrong!"

"The three of you are the ringleaders of that gang of rustlers and road agents that's been operating in these parts," Tilghman shouted. He wanted to make it very clear to anyone within earshot of his voice exactly what was going on here. "You've been hiding behind a lawman's badge just like your brother's been hiding behind being mayor! You're all under arrest!"

That bold declaration brought a burst of startled laughter from Dave Rainey.

"That's mighty big talk for a man who's as outnumbered as you are! You're the one who'd better give up! And if either of my brothers die, I'll see to it that you hang, mister!"

Dave was stubbornly keeping up the pose of being an honest lawman. Tilghman didn't know if he had done any good or not. But maybe some of the people of Burnt Creek would now begin to question what was really going on here. If they were to turn against Dave Rainey, that might tip the balance against the outlaws. Tilghman and Scanlon had to hold out for as long as they could and give that doubt time to work . . .

"Casey!" Scanlon suddenly exclaimed. "Casey, where are you?"

Tilghman glanced over his shoulder and saw Scanlon looking around frantically. Casey wasn't in the sitting room anymore, and she didn't answer Scanlon's calls. She had slipped out while Tilghman and Scanlon were concentrating on the danger in front of thcm.

"Where could she have – " Scanlon began.

At that moment, Cal Rainey made his move. Even wounded as bad as he was, all the fight hadn't left him. He lifted a foot, rested it on the window sill, and pushed back as hard as he could, driving his body into Tilghman's. Taken by surprise, Tilghman went over backward, sprawling on the floor as Cal twisted around and grappled with him for the Winchester.

At the same time, Cal shouted, "Dave! Rush 'em, Dave! Get in here and kill 'em all!"

Chapter 15

Without Cal being in the window to make the outlaws hold their fire, the barrage of rifle and pistol shots started up again, filling the air in the sitting room with hot lead. Scanlon had no choice but to hug the floor as bullets whined over his head.

A few feet away, Tilghman struggled desperately with Cal Rainey. Basically rendered one-armed by his wound, Cal fought with a berserk rage anyway. He wrenched the rifle away from Tilghman and smashed the stock against the lawman's jaw.

Tilghman shook off the blow and drove his left fist against Cal's injured shoulder. The rustler's face contorted in agony as he gasped out a curse and tried to slide his good hand down to the Winchester's action so he could fire it one-handed.

Tilghman hammered his right first against Cal's ear and drove him to the side. He got his other hand on the rifle barrel and shoved it upward just as Rainey found the trigger and jerked it. The bullet smashed into the ceiling and caused plaster to shower down around the battling men.

In close quarters like this, Cal couldn't cock the Winchester one-handed. He must have realized that because he let go of it and lunged for Tilghman's throat instead.

Tilghman blocked that grasping move and shot another punch into Cal's face. He didn't let up but struck again and again, bouncing the back of Cal's head against the floor until the rustler went limp.

By that time Scanlon was kneeling at the window again, jacking his Winchester's lever and firing swiftly as he called, "Here they come!"

Tilghman grabbed the other rifle and scrambled to the window, heedless of the bullets whipping around his head. Some of the rustlers had stayed where they were to provide covering fire, while the others charged toward the hotel.

Tilghman aimed at the men in the forefront of the attack and opened fire. One of the outlaws stumbled and went down, and Scanlon dropped another.

Then a bullet struck Tilghman's Winchester and ripped it out of his hands, leaving his fingers momentarily numb from the impact. He shook his right hand to get feeling back into it and reached for his Colt.

Down the hall, Raoul Gonzalez's scattergun boomed twice, but it was answered by a snarling burst of pistol fire. When Gonzalez didn't reload and fire again, Tilghman's heart sank a little. He figured the stableman had gone down under that withering attack up the rear stairs.

Tilghman drew in a deep breath and squared his shoulders as he faced the sitting room door and thumbed fresh shells into the Colt's empty chambers. This fight was nearly over, he sensed, but he was going to sell his life dearly and take as many of the lawless with him as he could.

He knew, too, that his death would be avenged. Marshal Nix had said that Chris Madsen and Heck Thomas would be coming along to Burnt Creek sooner or later, and when they did they would unleash hell and justice on any of the surviving outlaws.

It was too bad about Boone Scanlon, though. Tilghman had seen a core of goodness in the young man. Even with the things he had done as a member of the Rainey gang, Scanlon could have made something decent out of his life, if he'd had the chance.

Suddenly the gunfire outside the hotel intensified. Scanlon let out an excited whoop at the window.

"I see Coley Barnett down there!" he said. "Looks like he and some of the townsfolk are goin' after the gang."

Tilghman slid over to the window and ventured a glance out. Some of the outlaws had been caught in the middle of the street, and they were under fire from several different directions. Tilghman spotted Dave Rainey's lanky deputy kneeling behind a water barrel and cutting down on the outlaws with a rifle. Scanlon had been right about Coley Barnett. The deputy was fighting for the law against his former boss's gang.

More citizens were pouring lead into the building where some of the outlaws had holed up. The fighting was vicious, but Barnett had rallied a large force and now the rustlers were outnumbered.

Tilghman barely had time to appreciate that development before a rush of footsteps drew his attention back to his own predicament. The half-breed outlaw Garza lunged through the door, the gun in his hand spouting flame.

One of Garza's slugs tore up the floor next to Tilghman. The others smacked into the wall between the two windows.

Tilghman fired just one shot, but it punched deep into Garza's midsection, tearing through his guts and doubling him over. Garza's gun went off into the floor one more time as he fell.

Even as he collapsed, another outlaw took his place, but Scanlon was ready and knocked that man off his feet with a bullet to the chest.

The fact that the attack bottlenecked in the door worked in favor of Tilghman and Scanlon. Gun-thunder roared until it seemed to fill the entire world, and clouds of gunsmoke stung their noses and eyes as they fired again and again at the outlaws pouring through the door and piling up on the floor just inside the sitting room. Scanlon was hit but continued shooting until the hammer of his gun fell on an empty chamber. Tilghman fired his final shot an instant later and downed another of the enemy.

Even though Tilghman was half-deafened by

all the explosions, he heard the roar of a shotgun and saw one of the outlaws, who had been drawing a bead on him with a savage lccr on his face, thrown sideways by a load of buckshot that shredded flesh and pulped bone. The shotgun boomed again, and then rifle and pistol shots cracked in the corridor. The attackers disappeared as the fierce exchange continued for several hectic seconds.

The shooting stopped, leaving echoing silence in its place. Tilghman came to his feet, reloading, and he snapped the Colt's cylinder closed and raised the gun as a stocky figure appeared in the doorway.

"Señor Marshal!" Raoul Gonzalez exclaimed. "You are alive!"

"So are you, I see," Tilghman said wearily. The bloodstains on Gonzalez's shirt told him that the stableman was wounded, but Gonzalez clutched the smoking greener in both hands and a grin stretched across his face.

The tall, rangy figure of Coley Barnett appeared behind Gonzalez. The deputy has a bullet graze on his cheek that dripped blood, but otherwise he didn't seem to be hurt.

"Thank the Lord you fellas are all right!" he said. "I was afraid those varmints had done for you."

"They came mighty close," Tilghman said. "They would have, if it weren't for you and Raoul, Deputy, and the other folks who pitched in to help us."

"And that might not have happened if Casey Spencer hadn't risked life and limb gettin' to me so she could tell me what was really happenin'," Barnett said.

"Casey!"

That worried cry came from Scanlon, who was struggling to stand up. The side of his shirt was soaked with blood. Tilghman stepped over to him and took his arm to help him to his feet. He pulled Scanlon's shirt up and saw a deep, ugly graze, but he didn't think the wound was life-threatening.

"Where is she?" Scanlon went on. "Where's Casey?"

"She was at the jail the last time I saw her," Barnett explained. "That's where she found me."

"We'll get her, Boone," Tilghman said. "Don't worry."

He left Barnett to help Scanlon and went out into the hall, stepping over the bloody, sprawled bodies of several outlaws as he did so. Martin Rainey was still sitting in the chair where

Tilghman had left him tied up. The mayor's eyes were open wide, staring lifelessly. There were three bullet wounds in his chest.

"We didn't do that," Gonzalez said, nodding toward Martin's body. "His own men shot him by accident when they opened fire on the deputy and me."

Tilghman looked at the outlaw corpses littering the corridor and saw how it had played out. It had been Martin Rainey's bad luck to be caught helplessly between the two forces, and his men, desperate to escape the law closing in on them, hadn't been very careful with their shots.

That wasn't the way Tilghman would have wanted it, and certainly not the way he'd intended when he left Martin in the corridor, but he wasn't going to lose any sleep over what had happened to the man. According to Cal, Martin was the one who had come up with the idea of putting together the gang in the first place. It was in his mind that the plague of lawlessness around Burnt Creek had originated.

Live by the sword, die by the sword . . . or the six-gun.

Several more armed townsmen were waiting

in the hallway. They were the men Barnett had led up here to finish the job of wiping out the rustlers. Tilghman nodded to them and said, "I'm much obliged to you for your help, boys. Now there's one more thing you can do for me. Cal Rainey's in there, knocked out. If some of you could carry him over to the jail and lock him up . . . "

"We'll take care of it, Marshal, don't worry," one of the men said. "Putting that varmint behind bars has been a long time coming."

"Sooner or later the law catches up to those who deserve it, one way or the other," Tilghman said. "If I didn't believe that, I never would've pinned on a badge to start with."

Along with Scanlon, Barnett and Gonzalez, he went tiredly downstairs and through the hotel lobby. Somebody had led the horses out. Tilghman was trying to remember when the last time was that he had slept, and Scanlon was going on about how they needed to find Casey, as the four men stepped out onto the verandah.

"She's got to be around here somewhere," Barnett said. "Probably still at the jail."

As they turned in that direction, another thought occurred to Tilghman. He said, "What happened to Dave Rainey? Is he over there in the store where the rest of the bunch was cornered and wiped out?"

"I don't remember seein' him," Barnett said with a frown. "And he wasn't upstairs in the hotel, either."

That started alarm bells going off in Tilghman's brain. As he swung toward the jail, those bells were accompanied by a sudden scream. The crowd of people that had formed in the street once the fighting was over started to break apart fast as people scurried to get out of the way.

Tilghman found himself facing Dave Rainey. About twenty yards separated the two men.

But so did the frightened form of Casey Spencer, who was held tightly by Rainey's left arm around her neck while the renegade lawman's other hand pressed a gun barrel into her side.

Chapter 16

"Casey!" Boone Scanlon yelled as he started to lunge forward. Tilghman flung out an arm to stop him, and Barnett tightened his arm around his friend's shoulders.

"Tilghman!" Dave said. "I want my brothers. Bring them out here and let them go, or I'll kill this girl."

Moving deliberately, Tilghman stepped down from the hotel verandah to the street.

"I can't do that, Dave," he said as he started forward at a slow, steady pace. "Cal's wounded. He's going to be locked up and held for trial. I'm sorry to have to tell you that Martin's dead."

"Dead . . . ! You killed him!"

Tilghman shook his head.

"No, he caught some slugs from your own men during the fight upstairs. Justice had its own way of catching up to him. And it'll catch up to you, too, Dave, you know that. Don't make things any worse than thcy havc to be. Let Miss Spencer go."

"We would've wiped you out if it wasn't for her," Dave ranted. "She's the one who turned the town against me. Me! I'm the marshal of Burnt Creek!"

"You betrayed these folks by throwing in with your brothers on the rustling scheme," Tilghman said. He was still coming closer to Dave and Casey. "You see, the badge doesn't mean anything if the man behind it isn't worthy of wearing it."

"We tried to go straight." Dave Rainey's lips curled in a snarl. "We tried, damn it! It just never worked out."

"You gave up on the law too quick. Put the gun down. Don't make me kill you."

Dave's eyes dropped to the Colt on Tilghman's hip.

"Your gun's still in your holster! You can't beat me!"

Tilghman smiled faintly.

"Are you sure about that, Dave?"

For a split-second, his mind flashed back to the scene in front of that farmer's soddy, miles east of here, that had played out a few days earlier. He had faced a desperate, determined man there, too, and that hombre had been threatening a woman just like Dave Rainey was.

Could he save Casey, the way he had saved that farmer's wife?

Time seemed suspended. Then Rainey's face contorted with hate and his finger started to whiten on the trigger.

Tilghman's gun came out of its holster with lightning speed. It boomed and Rainey's head snapped back as the bullet bored through his brain. His gun slipped unfired from his fingers and he toppled backward, away from the trembling Casey Spencer, who flung herself forward and fell to her knees. Scanlon rushed into the street and gathered her in his arms, his own wound forgotten now.

Tilghman shoved Rainey's gun well out of reach with his boot, then stood over the fallen outlaw, still covering him. There was no need for that, he saw. His shot had been true, even though he hadn't taken the time to aim like he usually did. Dave Rainey was dead.

Before Tilghman had ever agreed to take the job as deputy U.S. marshal, he and Evett Nix had discussed the sort of man who ought to be wearing that badge. Tilghman had told Nix his theory about how it was the man who was careful and took his time who won most gunfights. A good lawman had to be reluctant to draw his weapon.

But, Tilghman thought as he pouched his iron, sometimes he could still be fast on the draw when he really needed to.

* * *

Burnt Creek was still cleaning up that afternoon, following the battle, when two men rode into town. Tilghman was sitting on the porch in front of the marshal's office – Coley Barnett's office now, since the town council had offered him the job of marshal and he had accepted – when he spotted the riders coming along the street. He stood up to greet them, his tall, rangy frame unfolding from the chair.

One of the newcomers was well-dressed, with sleek dark hair under his hat. His clothes were carefully brushed and didn't show much trail dust.

The other man was shorter and stockier, wearing clothes that looked like they'd been slept in every night for a week. A battered old hat perched on his rumpled thatch of hair, and a ragged soup strainer mustache drooped over his mouth. He spoke first, saying to Tilghman, "I heard a lot of hammerin' comin' from behind the undertaker's place when we rode by. Sounded to me like he was buildin' a bunch of coffins. When I heard that, I said it sounded like ol' Tilghman had been hard at work here. I said that, didn't I, Heck?"

"You did, Chris," the dark-haired man agreed. "And to tell you the truth, I thought the same thing. Keeping the undertaker busy planting owlhoots, eh, Bill?"

"Well, that wasn't my intention," Tilghman said. "You know I'd rather take prisoners and let the courts deal with them." He shrugged. "Sometimes it just doesn't work out that way."

"No, it doesn't," Deputy U.S. Marshal Heck Thomas agreed.

"Still, you could've waited for us," Deputy U.S. Marshal Chris Madsen added. "Nix told you he'd send us along to give you a hand as soon as we got back from that other job."

Tilghman propped a shoulder against one of the posts holding up the awning over the boardwalk and drawled, "Well, if I'd known you boys were going to show up today, I'd have tried to hold off on starting the ball."

Thomas glanced at the front wall of the hotel, which must have had a thousand bullet holes all over its top floor, and said dryly, "Looks like it was quite a fandango."

"Did you leave any of 'em alive?" Madsen asked.

Tilghman pointed over his shoulder with a thumb.

"One of the ringleaders is locked up inside. The new town marshal and his deputy will take care of him and hold him for trial. Of course, that deputy is laid up for a few days because he was wounded in this little dust-up, but he'll be all right."

Coley Barnett wasn't the only one with a new job. Tilghman had done something that really went against the grain for him: he had allowed Boone Scanlon to go free, with a solemn promise from the young man that he would stay on the right side of the law from now on. His job as deputy marshal of Burnt Creek would help see to that.

And Casey would make sure of it, especially after their wedding, which would take place as soon as Scanlon was on his feet again.

Madsen and Thomas swung down from their saddles and looped their reins around the hitch

166

rail in front of the marshal's office.

"I reckon you'll tell us all about it?" Thomas said.

"Sure, if you want to hear the story. The hotel dining room is still open, even though their best waitress is playing nursemaid right now, and they make a good cup of coffee."

Tilghman started across the street, and Thomas and Madsen fell in alongside him.

Three guardians of the law, ready for whatever challenges the wild Oklahoma Territory might have for them.

Author's Note

Although the events in this novel are fictional, they're loosely based on several incidents that occurred in the career of William Tilghman, who really did have an illustrious history as an Old West lawman, serving as deputy sheriff, sheriff, city marshal, chief of police, and deputy U.S. marshal. He wore a lawman's badge, off and on, for more than forty years, and his adventurous life stretched all the way from his days as a buffalo hunter to a stint as writer and director of early silent motion pictures. For more information about this veteran frontiersman, see the excellent, highly readable biography BILL TILGHMAN: MARSHAL OF THE LAST FRONTIER by Floyd Miller.

About the Author

A lifelong Texan, James Reasoner has been a professional writer for more than thirty years. In that time, he has authored several hundred novels and short stories in numerous genres. James is best known for his Westerns, historical novels, and war novels, he is also the author of two mystery novels that have achieved cult classic status, TEXAS WIND and DUST DEVILS. Writing under his own name and various pseudonyms, his novels have garnered praise from Publishers Weekly, Booklist, and the Los Angeles Times, as well as appearing on the New York Times and USA Today bestseller lists. His website is www.jamesreasoner.com

MISSING

From Aurora, Illinois

Timmothy Pitzen

6-year-old Timmothy Pitzen, date of birth October 18, 2004, is missing from Aurora, Illinois but was last seen at a water park in Wisconsin Dells, Wisconsin on May 12, 2011. He was last known to be in the company of his mother who has since been found deceased in Rockford, Illinois. Timmothy may go by the nickname Tim or Timmy and is described as 4'2" tall with brown eyes, brown hair, and weighing 70 pounds. Anyone with information is asked to call Aurora Police Department (Illinois) at **1-630-256-5000, 1 800 THE MISSING or 911**.

facebook.com/help.find.Timmothy

NOTE: AURORA, ILLINOIS -- One year after 6-year-old Timmothy Pitzen disappeared, Aurora police released new surveillance video of his mother checking and leaving a Wisconsin resort. On May 11, 2011, Amy Fry-Pitzen took her only son out of Greenman Elementary School in Aurora early on the school day. Without telling any family members, Timmothy and Amy went on a three-day, 500-mile road trip, stopping at zoos and water parks. On the third day, Amy finally called family to report that she was fine. Timmothy was heard in the background. Police found her body and a suicide note the next morning. Timmothy has not been found.

Also available from Western Fictioneers

The Traditional West

The classic American Western returns in this huge collection of brand-new stories by some of the top Western writers in the world today.

Six-guns and Slay Bells:
A Creepy Cowboy Christmas

Put on your Santa hat and saddle up for this collection of creepy Christmas stories from the Western Fictioneers, the world's only organization of professional authors devoted solely to Western fiction.

The Peacemakers

Collections of 4 award winning western stories in each volume

Volume I, Volume II, & Volume III

The Wolf Creek series:

Here you will find many of your favorite authors, working together as Ford Fargo to weave a complex and textured series of Old West adventures like no one has ever seen.

Book 1: Bloody Trail

Also available from Western Fictioneers

Book 2: Kiowa Vengeance

Book 3: Murder in Dogleg City

Book 4: The Taylor County War

And More Wolf Creek to Come

The Western Fictioneers Library

RAW DEAL AT PASCO SPRINGS by Clay More

LEAVING KANSAS by Frank Roderus

JUDGE ON THE RUN by Clay More

RANGER'S REVENGE by James J. Griffin

REACHING COLORADO by Frank Roderus

DEATH STALKS THE RANGERS by James J. Griffin

A ROPE FOR SCUDDER by Clay More

COMING: The Western Fictioneers Library

DEAD MAN'S GUN AND OTHER WESTERN STORIES by Ed Gorman

GUN FOR HIRE by Jory Sherman

FINDING NEVADA by Frank Roderus

THE CAST-IRON STAR AND OTHER WESTERN STORIES by Robert J. Randisi

HOME TO TEXAS by Frank Roderus

BUZZARD BAIT by Jory Sherman

STAMPEDE AT RATTLESNAKE PASS by Clay More

CHARLIE AND THE SIR by Frank Roderus

JASON EVERS: HIS OWN STORY by Frank Roderus

POTTER'S FIELDS by Frank Roderus

THE TRAIL BROTHERS by Troy D. Smith

DOUBLE-DEALING AT DIRTVILLE by Clay More

HIS ROYAL HIGHNESS, J. AUBREY WHITFORD by Frank Roderus

CPSIA information can be obtained at www.ICGtesting.com
Printed in the USA
LVOW10s1708300913

354764LV00015B/1107/P